READY FOR REBELLION

"You're going to meet your twin brother, Tom."

Eddie just stared at him. The old man was no jokester. "Tom? My twin brother?"

"This is going to be a lot for you to take in, but try to follow me. Twelve years ago, when you and Tom were born, you were separated. For your safety. Tom stayed on EarthOne, you came here. Now it's time."

Eddie's head hurt. He was confused. "Time for what?"

"To meet each other. To switch places. To learn about each other's home planets. To get ready for the rebellion to save the Earths."

"What about football? I'm the captain."

Grandpa smiled. He reached out and ran a hand through Eddie's short hair. "*We* need captains, too. Let's go. We don't have much time."

THE TWINNING PROJECT

ROBERT LIPSYTE

HOUGHTON MIFFLIN HARCOURT
Boston New York

TO THE NEWEST STAR,
DANIEL ALEX NACHUMI

The text of this book is set in Monotype Apollo.
Book design by Sharismar Rodriguez

The Library of Congress has cataloged the hardcover edition as follows:
Lipsyte, Robert.
The twinning project / by Robert Lipsyte.
p. cm.
Summary: Tom and Eddie, identical twins and mirror opposites living on two different
Earths some fifty years apart, must switch places and identities to thwart the alien scientists
who threaten their planets.
[1. Space and time—Fiction. 2. Middle schools—Fiction. 3. Schools—Fiction. 4. Twins—
Fiction. 5. Science fiction.] I. Title.
PZ7.L67Tw 2012
[Fic]—dc23
2011050252

ISBN: 978-0-547-64571-1 hardcover
ISBN: 978-0-544-22522-0 paperback

Manufactured in the United States of America
DOC 10 9 8 7 6 5 4 3 2 1
4500484038

BAD ENOUGH

ONE

I DON'T fit in at school because I don't do what I'm told if it's stupid. I don't keep my mouth shut when I have something to say. I don't let bullies push me around. And I can't just stand there and watch bullies pick on other kids. That's how I got kicked out of my last middle school.

I was in the cafeteria minding my own business but keeping my eyes unstuck, as usual. You have to stay alert. I was eating at one of the tables back near the trash cans. The zombies call kids who eat at those tables losers, dorks, orcs, humps, trolls, Goths, stoners—you know, because they can't stand people who aren't undead like them.

I call us rebels.

This was on a Friday before a football game, and there was a pep rally going on in the center of the cafeteria. I can't understand why middle school kids play football. Jocks are dumb enough already. They don't need their brains banged around more. The jocks yelled, their girlfriends danced, and the zombies clapped. At the rebel tables we pretended to ignore them.

One of the jock bullies noticed that we weren't clapping, so he walked over with that jock-bully walk, toes pointed in, shoulders rolling, and said, "Where's your school spirit?"

The rebels froze up and looked down.

This is a problem. It takes a lot to get rebels to do something as a group. Rebels need leaders, but they have trouble following one. They're rebels.

The jock bully picked up a tray from our table and let the food slide down on a kid's head. Spaghetti and chocolate pudding. The jocks and their girlfriends cheered, and the zombies clapped harder. The teachers pretended they were too busy on their BlackBerries to notice. Teachers let jocks get away with stuff. Maybe they're afraid of them, too.

I recognized the bully, a guy who was always slamming into kids' shoulders in the hall. He wasn't even a good football player. Typical.

He picked up two more full trays and started strutting around the table, balancing them on his palms. He kept turning his head to make sure the jerks at the jock tables were watching. They whistled and pounded their feet as he circled my table deciding whom he would trash next.

I waited until he was three steps away before I slipped out my TPT GreaseShot IV. It's about as big as a pencil flashlight: the smallest cordless grease gun you can buy online. It has an electronic pulse and can be set for semi- or full automatic. I had only one chance and I'd never used the grease gun in combat before. I put it on full automatic.

He was about a foot away when he turned his head again back toward the jock tables. That's when I fired grease in front of his red LeBron X South Beach sneakers.

The right sneaker hit the grease puddle, slid, and went up in the air.

He went down in slow motion.

It was funny. I was thinking, *Too bad nobody's shooting this.*

Too bad, somebody was.

You can see it on YouTube.

The two trays rose off his palms. He was howling like a dog as the veggie tacos, burgers, fries, and drinks avalanched onto his head. Then his left sneaker slid into the grease and he was lifted completely off the floor.

Kids were screaming as he slammed down on his back, arms out. I'm not sure exactly what happened next because that part wasn't on YouTube and I was moving out.

I try not to hang around the scene of my paybacks. It's a sure way to get caught—standing around looking like you're waiting for applause.

It didn't matter. The YouTube clip shows that the person shooting the grease gun was wearing the same blue Bach Off! hoodie I was wearing that day.

It was a zero-tolerance school.

TWO

Zero tolerance?

I have to explain everything to Eddie. It's not because he's slow or because he's a jock, even though he is slow and he is a jock. It's because, even though our planets are similar in most ways, there's one big difference: His planet is at least fifty years behind Earth. He calls his planet Earth, too, which is confusing. I call his planet EarthTwo because it's younger than my Earth.

Eddie and I are identical twins, born a minute apart. I'm the older one, like my planet.

I beamed a thought at him: *Zero tolerance means one strike and you're out. You're toast. Forked. Expelled.*

Not fair, Tommy. People deserve second chances. You had a good reason. You were protecting other kids.

Tell it to the principal.

Maybe I will. When I come to visit.

Eddie says things like that to tease me. Well, the truth is I put words like that in his mouth to tease myself. It's one thing to stand in the backyard having an imaginary conversation with your imaginary twin on an imaginary planet. It's another thing to imagine the two of you together for real. How great would that be? A best friend who's your twin brother? That's not imagination. That's being insane.

So what's up, pup?

Eddie's always coming up with these bizarro old-fashioned expressions. Sometimes I Google them. They're always expressions that were cool in the twentieth century.

No big deal, Eddie. I've been expelled before. I get to stay home for a few days, read, run some games, play my violin.

It's so groovy you can do stuff like that. I'd just practice my jump shot.

I don't even have a jump shot.

I'll show you. It's easy, not like playing the violin or reading. So, what happens after a few days?

Mom comes up with a new school for me, and I go back to the land of the undead.

Think positive, Tommy. I know you'll find a school that appreciates you. You are one special cat.

Dad always said, "Nobody's special."

Yeah, but Dad always said, "Everybody's special."

I miss him.

Me, too. That's why we've got to keep remembering him.

The back door slammed. "Who's out there?"

It was the Lump, Mom's tenant. He acts like it's his house.

I must have been talking out loud again. Eddie and I usually talk inside my head, but sometimes I get carried away and treat Eddie like he's real.

Gotta go, bro. It's the Lump.

Give him a chance. Find the good in him. Get him on your team.

That's Eddie. A good guy. My opposite.

THREE

FROM the first day at my next new middle school, I could tell that the psychologist, Dr. Traum, was out to get me. It was hate at first sight. He looked at me so hard, I could feel the nasty rays off his big green eyes. He leaned across his desk and waved papers in my face.

"This is your third middle school, Thomas. Third. What makes you think you'll fit in here?"

I shrugged. *How should I know? And why would I want to fit into your stupid zombie school?*

"Look at these test scores. Obviously, you are smart. Very smart. So why do you keep disappointing people?"

They love that word, "disappoint." It's supposed to make you feel bad.

I never feel bad.

I *am* bad.

As if he was reading my mind, Dr.
It sounded like a bus sneezing when it l
disabled people. I'd been through this k
sation before. *Next he'll tell me he's goin*
chance.

"I am going to give you a chance, Thomas."

Against his better judgment.

"It's against my better judgment, of course. But I think there's good in you, Thomas, and we'll find it together."

I looked right into his eyes. "I won't disappoint you," I lied.

He leaned back in his chair and stared at me. He was wearing jeans and running shoes without laces and a T-shirt with some old-time rock band's name on it. The Clash. Old guys who dress like kids are the worst phonies in the world. And they're sneaky. They want you to think that because they dress like you, they're on your side. And that you can trust them.

You can never trust them.

Dr. Traum lowered his voice. "Did you ever consider that the boy who fell in the cafeteria because of you could have been seriously hurt?"

"No," I said.

It was true. I hadn't thought about it. I didn't care. He was a bully. He deserved whatever happened to him.

as that because it just never occurred to you or
ause you didn't care?"

"Yes," I said.

He didn't react to my not answering him. He was acting cool.

"One more thing." He waved a paper. "Says here you
blow a wicked fiddle."

I hate it when old guys try to sound hip. I nodded. "I
played first violin in my last school."

"It remains to be seen if you are good enough for
Nearmont Middle School. Just so happens, I run the orchestra here."

Groovy.

FOUR

ALESSA was nervous when the new school psychologist called her into his office. She thought she was finished seeing shrinks. Mom and Dad had promised. As long as she stayed on her diet and practiced cello every day, there would be no more sessions and no more pills.

"Alessa!" He didn't look like any shrink she'd ever seen: a short, skinny white man in jeans and a T-shirt. A ponytail. He looked happy to see her, his big green eyes sparkling. "Thank you for coming. I'm Dr. Traum."

He waved her to a couch along one wall and sat down on a hard chair next to it. She started to wedge herself into a corner of the couch, the way she did for the shrinks, then stopped herself and plopped down on her butt.

Oh, Lessi, she thought, *this is so uncool.*

Dr. Traum just looked at her, smiling, until she blurted out, "What did I do wrong?"

Even uncool-er.

He frowned. "Oh, no. Nothing wrong at all. I need your help."

"Me? Help you?"

"If you would. There's a new student in school. I want to be sure he gets off on the right foot here. I'd like you to be his mentor, his guide. His name is Thomas Canty."

"The YouTube guy?"

"He's had problems in other schools, to be sure. He's an excellent violinist. I'd like you to make him feel at home in the orchestra, too."

Alessa wanted to say, *You've got the wrong girl, Doc. I've got enough problems guiding myself.* But the chance to help somebody interested her. Nobody had ever asked her to do that before.

"What should I do?"

"Just be his friend. And if anything seems, well, odd to you, let me know so I can help him."

"What kind of odd?"

Dr. Traum got closer. His face was very smooth. No wrinkles for such an old dude. Botox, like Mom? "This has to be between just us, Alessa . . . Thomas's father died several years ago. It was very difficult for him. Sometimes he thinks he hears voices. I want to know about it."

"You want me to spy on him?"

"I want you to help me help him. You wouldn't want anything bad to happen to him because we didn't reach out, would you?" Dr. Traum stood up. "Can I count on you, Alessa?"

"I'll try."

"That's all I ask. Thanks so much. You may go back to class."

Alessa had to heave herself up from the soft couch. *I've got to do those exercises,* she thought.

Outside the office, she wondered if Dr. Traum should have told her all that stuff about Thomas Canty. Wasn't that private? But she was excited about being a mentor, a guide. Maybe even a friend.

FIVE

By the time I had filled out all the papers, it was lunchtime. I wasn't sure where to sit after I got my food. You have to be careful where you start off sitting because you can get stuck there.

I was pretending I knew where I was going while I scoped the tables. It was the usual: jocks . . . fashion girls . . . thugs . . . brainiacs — you know. I spotted the rebel tables just as a big fat girl stood up at one of them and waved at me. Next to her was a guy with black eye makeup and a girl with green hair, both wearing big "Save the Earth" buttons. I could get into that environmental stuff if the tree huggers weren't such know-it-all spazzes.

I walked over slowly, checking out the big girl who had waved at me. She'd been reading on her laptop. When I got closer, I could see it was something about

Twilight. Not even the stupid vampire book itself, but something *about* it. Like it was so important you needed to *study* it.

It's major to get the first words in. "Bad enough to read that toxic waste, but to read *about* it?"

Her head jerked a little, like I'd jabbed her. Then she said, "You've got to know your enemy."

That was something my dad would say, so I was interested. "Vampires are your enemy?"

"They don't exist."

"So why are you reading about them?"

"Because the idea of them exists. People believe in them."

"Stupid people," I snapped.

"Exactly," she said. "You've got to understand what stupid people believe so you can understand the world we live in."

I dug her right away. She was no dummy. But I stayed cool. "I might be able to get behind that."

Then she said, "So what did that kid on YouTube actually do to you?"

"Actually," I said, mocking her serious tone of voice, "nothing."

Everybody at the table was looking at me. I don't think they believed me.

"So why did you do it?" She was intense.

"He was a bully," I said.

"But he wasn't *your* bully," she said.

"Every bully," I said, "is *your* bully."

The way she looked at me, I was afraid she was going to hug me. The other kids at the table all looked at each other with these dorky looks, rolling their eyes, lifting a corner of their lips. But I could tell they liked what I said. Not that I cared.

"I'm Alessa," she said. "I can show you around the school."

"Sounds like a plan. I'm Tom."

SIX

A FTER Dr. Traum heard me play, he patted my shoulder and put me in with the first violins. He said if I did everything he told me, I'd get to play a solo at the winter concert. I thought, *Big whoop.* That's an Eddie expression.

I'm an okay fiddler. I started when I was three. Dad played the violin, and we loved to play together. We played everything—Mozart, bluegrass, the Beatles. I kept playing after he disappeared so I could imagine he was still there next to me.

Every time I practiced, I warmed up with a couple of minutes of the dueling-violins number from *Riverdance.* We'd seen it on TV once, and Dad and I loved whaling away, especially when he'd come home from one of his trips coaching star violinists. We didn't do the dances, but we always ended up laughing. And then Dad would get serious and hug me around the shoulders. When I was smaller, he'd drop to his knees and touch his forehead to mine. Sometimes I thought he could tell what I was thinking.

Dr. Traum was new at the orchestra job, and he left the musicians alone. I had the feeling he didn't know that much about music. Alessa was the only cello player in school who was bigger than the cello. She wasn't very good.

My classes were all right. I like school, at least the learning part, not the having-to-get-along-with-other-people part. Math is math, you're right or you're wrong, and the books we were reading in English were okay, especially *The Prince and the Pauper,* by Mark Twain, my all-time favorite, which I've read lots of times. It's about a poor boy with a bad father and a rich boy who's on his way to becoming king of England. They switch lives for a while. The poor boy's name was Tom Canty, like mine, which is why I named my imaginary twin after the prince, Edward Tudor.

Science has hardcore information you can use. How else do you think I learned to make stink bombs? French is memory. So is music. I have a good memory. In tech lab, the controls on the computers were easy to bypass, so I could surf the web looking for new tech gadgets and bomb recipes.

We hardly ever had gym, maybe because there were so many fat kids in school or maybe because the gym teachers were only interested in the jocks. That was okay with me. I've never played much ball because I don't like teams. Anyway, I'm not into sports. That's Eddie territory. He's good at every sport. We're mirror twins. Opposites.

That first week at Nearmont we played dodgeball, the meanest game ever invented. I hate it. It's like a training game for bullies. This one kid, a huge kid with a lot of pimples on his forehead, Todd Britzky, would yell, "Britzkyball!" and pick out someone slow or fat or scared, then fire away. He nailed Alessa hard. The gym teacher was busy on his iPhone, probably doing stuff for some varsity team.

I watched Britzky. He had that jock-bully walk, but I could tell he really didn't have much confidence in himself. He looked over his shoulder a lot, and his eyes flicked around. I figured I'd have to find a way to mess with his mind; he was making Alessa miserable, and she was trying to help me learn my way around school. But I didn't have time. I had to act fast.

I slipped the grease gun out of my pocket and up my sleeve and walked out on the gym floor. When Britzky heaved the ball toward me, I batted it away.

"You're out," he said.

"You're roadkill, pizza face," I said.

He got so red, his pimples lit up. Kids started stamping their feet. Britzky didn't know what to do. He knew he had to do something or he'd lose his bullyhood, but he probably knew my reputation from YouTube. I stood my ground, waiting for him to charge. I slipped the grease gun into full automatic.

A hand closed around mine. It was Dr. Traum's. What was he doing here? Following me?

"You have to obey the rules, Thomas," he whispered. "You're not a special person here."

"Nobody's special, and everybody's special," I said, remembering my last conversation with Eddie. I always love to quote Dad.

Dr. Traum looked at me hard, blinked, and nodded. "I've heard that before."

He opened my fist and took the grease gun. I waited to hear him tell me I was expelled or at least suspended. But he walked out of the gym without looking back. Maybe he really needed another first violinist.

SEVEN

EDDIE Tudor thought the new football coach was a kook. He didn't seem to know that much about football, and at practice he didn't wear sweats and a ball cap, like most coaches. Instead, he wore a shiny pale green suit. It was almost a zoot suit. The pants were pegged and stitched up the sides. The shoulders of the jacket were so big, it looked as though he was wearing football pads, and the lapels were wide, almost like wings. He wore a white shirt and a skinny purple tie.

The guys on the team thought he was trying too hard to look hip, but Eddie told them to give him a chance, since he was new, and maybe he was just trying hard to make a good impression. Eddie was the captain, so if there was a problem with the new coach, it would be his job to represent his teammates. No sweat. He liked being Captain Eddie.

One day the week before, the school psychologist suddenly quit, and so did the football coach. The next day Dr. Traum arrived to take over both jobs. Eddie was trying to like him. He was the coach. But it wasn't easy.

Now it was Dr. Traum's first game at Nearmont Junior High, and he didn't know all the players or all the plays in the playbook. Eddie stood on the sidelines waiting to go back into the game. He told himself to concentrate, to forget about Dr. Traum.

Eddie loved football. He was the quarterback. He thought the best feeling in the world was during those wonderful few seconds when the ball was in your hand and the entire field was spread out in front of you, waiting for you to make your play.

At that moment, he truly felt like Captain Eddie, powerful, in charge, a prince of the universe. Time stood still as he watched the opposing players rushing toward him, growling like attack dogs ready to pounce. He would dance out of their way until he spotted one of his teammates in the clear, and then he'd throw the ball.

And he loved the crowd, loved hearing them whistle and yell. The new cheerleader, Merlyn, had a way of whipping her head from side to side so that her long black hair looked like a flag snapping in the wind. The crowd chanted "Touch-down" or "Dee-fense" in rhythm with her magical hair. Her voice, sweet and silvery, knifed through the crowd noise.

Sometimes, Eddie imagined Dad in the crowd. Dad had seen him play PeeWee football, but he was gone before Eddie made the junior high varsity as a seventh-grader. He was the starting quarterback! Dad would have been so proud. He always said Eddie would be a great quarterback someday.

And Dad would know. He traveled a lot, all year long, giving private coaching lessons to star college and professional quarterbacks.

Dr. Traum banged Eddie's shoulder pads, waking him out of his thoughts about Dad. "You ready, Eddie?"

"Ready, Coach."

"Okay, Eddie, let's go," Dr. Traum said. "Blue seventeen."

"That play's not working, Coach. They're reading it."

"I said, 'Blue seventeen,' Eddie."

Eddie ran out on the field and waited for the huddle to form around him. Blue seventeen was a pass-action play. He was supposed to pretend to hand off to a running back before he stepped back to pass. It was a good play when it worked, but it hadn't been working all game. The other team was supposed to pause while it tried to figure out whether Eddie was really handing it off or faking it, which was supposed to give him a couple of extra seconds. But the fake hadn't fooled them, and that was why Nearmont was twelve points behind in the fourth quarter. Eddie didn't want to do it, but if Coach said so . . .

"Red nine, fourteen, green twenty-three, eight, blue seventeen."

The ball came back into his hands. He turned, bent over, and pretended to hand it to the best running back on the team. He wanted to *really* hand it off—a better play—but Coach said . . .

Coach is wrong.

You're supposed to obey Coach.

I'm the captain.

Just do it!

Eddie stepped back to throw, the ball in both hands under his chin, the way Dad had taught him. He pulled his right arm back, elbow bent. While he stretched out his left arm, pointing left, he looked to the right, hoping to confuse the other team. He dropped his right shoulder, snapped his throwing arm forward, and stepped down on his left foot. He twisted his wrist and fingers as he let go and followed through with his empty hand facing the ground.

Just before he let go, he heard the other coach scream,

"Put a hat on him!" and he spotted a slight movement out of the corner of his left eye. It was too late to react.

A helmet slammed into his chest, and he hit the ground hard, no time to roll into a ball. His head slammed into the ground.

Lights blinked off, like a power failure in a thunderstorm.

When they came on again, Eddie could hear his pal Ronnie yelling from the stands, "Eddie! Eddie!"

The coach was looking down at him. "You okay?"

"Just got my bell rung." His head hurt, but he didn't want to leave the game. "Did he catch it?"

"How many?" Dr. Traum held up some fingers. They were blurry.

Eddie guessed. "Two?"

"Close enough. Blue seventeen. They'll never expect it again."

He opened his mouth to say, *They always expect it. It's all you know.*

But Eddie never talked back to a coach. He shut his mouth and got up.

EIGHT

DAD and I talked about history all the time. He was into empires—the Roman and the Mongol, the Russian and British, and the Han Dynasty in China. He said Americans had better study those empires if they expected to survive. Dad had a saying that went something like, "People who forget history repeat the bad stuff."

I wanted to like my new history class, but the teacher, Mrs. Rupp, spoiled it. She had this thing she called Mrs. Rupp's Timeline, with all the dates she thought were important from ancient times to the present. She said that the best way to understand important events was by memorizing her timeline, so you would know the order in which things happened. I could understand that you should know there were almost a hundred years between the Revolutionary War and the Civil War, but I hated wasting time memorizing dates. I liked to read about dinosaurs and the Roman Empire and Custer's Last Stand and the civil rights movement, but I hated to memorize the dates. Math, French, and music you have to memorize, but not history. History should be stories about real people. Dad said so.

My first week, Mrs. Rupp made the class memorize "Great Dates in Science and Technology," like when the telephone was invented and when Earth conquered outer space. She tried to make it into some kind of demento game show we should be thrilled to play.

"Oh-kay-doh-kay, here we go," she shouted. "It's time for . . . Mrs. Rupp's Timeline!"

She cranked up her laptop, and a picture of a spaceship with a hammer-and-sickle emblem flashed on the wall. "We haven't heard from our newest student, Tom . . . Canty! Let's break it out for Tom."

The class applauded, but they were sarcastic claps. They didn't like memorizing dates, either. Or maybe they just didn't like me. I'm oh-kay-doh-kay with that.

"Let's have the day . . . month . . . year when the first rocket ship orbited the Earth."

"That was *Sputnik,*" I said. "It was a Russian satellite, and it really freaked out America. We were afraid they would use it to—"

"Thank you, Tom," said Mrs. Rupp in that tone

teachers use when they want you to feel so brainless that you'll shut up. "Now, what's the answer I'm looking for? Day . . . month . . . year."

A girl with long dark hair that covered most of her face raised her hand. Mrs. Rupp said, "Let's hear from another new student. Merlyn?"

Merlyn stood up and said, "The fourth of October, 1957." She had a sweet, silvery voice.

"Excellent, Merlyn. Got that, Tom?"

I said, "It was important because America and Russia were enemies and—"

"Thank you for sharing, Tom, but that's not today's takeaway."

I couldn't stop myself. "It was a big deal, it changed history, it—"

Mrs. Rupp glared at me. "Maybe you should be teaching this class, Tom."

"Excellent idea," I said. I stood up, and Alessa pulled on my sleeve.

Lucky for Mrs. Rupp, the bell rang. I was ready to give a lecture on how we hated the Russians back in the 1950s and what a waste that was. Dad told me all about it.

The next class was orchestra, and I was looking forward to getting lost in the music. I could shut out everything in my life, even the scratchy out-of-tune violins around me, and hear only myself. I was thinking about the music, and I didn't notice Britzky rush out of Mrs. Rupp's class ahead of me. He was waiting for me in the hall when I walked out.

He looked wild. "You think you're so smart!" he shouted.

"Tom, watch out!" screamed Alessa. She was right behind me.

Britzky charged me. I jumped out of the way, but Alessa didn't move fast enough, and he slammed into her.

"Mind your business, whale-butt," he growled at her.

I helped Alessa pick up her music books. She wouldn't look at me because she was crying.

Too bad, I thought. *I might have liked it here at this school for a while. But now I have to do something about Britzky.*

It would probably get me expelled again.

NINE

THE night before I did something about Britzky, I rode my bike over to Grandpa's nursing home in time for dessert. It's against the rules for visitors to eat there without advance notice, except for me when I bring my violin and play with Grandpa, who plays the piano. He can still do that, except if you ask him to play Mozart, you might get some old song like "Moon River."

He was glad to see me and gave me a big hug. "Who are you?"

"Tom, your grandson. John's son."

"John." He smiled. "He was here yesterday."

I wish. Dad disappeared two years ago when the small plane he was on crashed into a lake. He was on his way to give a violin master class. Everybody was saved except Dad. His body was never found.

"Want to play?" I said.

"Chess?"

"Music."

"What do I play?"

I led him over to the piano. We got applause before I even took my violin out of its padded backpack. Grandpa surprised me by starting Beethoven's Sonata no. 1. Then he suddenly switched to a song from *South Pacific*. It was fun trying to keep up with him. He played tunes from other Broadway shows. I was sorry after a half hour or so when he got tired and quit.

Dessert was great. Chocolate cake with vanilla ice cream. Old ladies kept coming over to our table to pinch my cheek and rub Grandpa's back.

Grandpa leaned over to me. "Listen up." He put his mouth close to my ear and whispered, "Stay on your toes. It's crunch time. The monitors have landed."

I felt sad. Poor Grandpa. Sometimes I thought he was my only friend in the world—at least the only nonimaginary one—and he was old and crazy. I hugged him and told him I had to get home.

He said loud enough for all the old ladies to hear, "Come back soon, John."

TEN

NEARMONT, N.J.
2011

BOTH cars were in the driveway when I got home, and there were lights on in the kitchen and living room. I didn't want to have to talk to Mom or the Lump. I rode around to the back of the house and into the little stone garden that nobody ever used except me. I leaned my bike against a tree and waited for Eddie.

Sometimes it takes a while for the clouds to open up so I can spot the double stars in Eddie's galaxy. Until there's a clear path through the sky between us, we can't send our thought beams.

I know this sounds insane, which is why I don't talk about it. It all began about two years ago.

The summer Dad disappeared, Mom was a wreck and I hung out with Grandpa. His mind was fine then. We'd sit in the stone garden and take turns reading books to each other. Grandpa's favorite author was Mark Twain.

Grandpa said everything you need to know about how the world works and how people act was in Mark Twain's books. He said Dad thought so, too.

First, we read *The Adventures of Tom Sawyer,* which I liked, and then *Adventures of Huckleberry Finn,* which I liked even better. Huck was a rebel. Next we read *The Prince and the Pauper,* and then *A Connecticut Yankee in King Arthur's Court,* which I liked even though it was too long and I didn't understand everything without Grandpa's help. It was about a guy who goes back in time to fight knights and dragons. He defeats some bad guys by predicting an eclipse of the sun, which he knew was going to happen because he was from the future and had studied history and remembered the date. Mrs. Rupp would love that.

Grandpa's number-one all-time favorite Mark Twain book was *The Mysterious Stranger.* In that book, the devil comes down to Earth and explains the human race to a couple of boys my age. It's almost like Mark Twain was on the devil's side.

Grandpa and Dad always told me to use my imagination instead of just believing what I was told. They said that Twain made up stuff that was truer than most of what you learned in school.

It was during that summer hanging out with Grandpa after Dad disappeared that I started using my imagination to keep from feeling so bad. I came up with the idea of a twin brother.

In my fantasy, Eddie and I were separated at birth to save us from the aliens who secretly ran Earth. (We were truly separated—we had been connected at the butt!) Then I came up with a great story to explain it. These aliens were scientists who had created two Earths as an experiment. I stayed on the first Earth they had created, while Eddie was sent to the newer planet, EarthTwo, which is almost like Earth but fifty years younger. But the experiment wasn't working out because humans were messing up their planets, poisoning the water and the air, dropping bombs on each other, and letting kids die of diseases that could be wiped out. The aliens were thinking seriously about blowing up one or even both planets.

Sounds silly, I guess, but talking to Eddie always made me feel better when things were lousy, and I was lonely after Dad disappeared, especially whenever I got kicked out of school. Even though Eddie was a jock, he never said anything mean to me. He never made me feel bad. After I saw *Star Wars,* I decided that I was Eddie's dark side.

I have a pink scar on my left butt cheek from an operation I had when I was a baby. Mom said it was a growth that had to be removed. I like to pretend it's the scar from where Eddie and I were connected when we were born.

Whenever I had a mysterious pain, like a headache or a stomachache or what felt like a sudden twisted ankle even though I was just playing the violin, I would imagine that something had happened to Eddie. Maybe his ankle twisted coming down wrong after snagging a rebound. Besides being a quarterback, Eddie was point guard on his junior high school basketball team and a starting pitcher when he was wasn't playing the outfield on the baseball team. The pains never lasted long. They were like news flashes keeping me up to date on Eddie. The worst was a pain in my butt cheek one time, like someone had drilled me with a baseball.

Next time we talked, Eddie told me that's exactly what had happened. He had lost a game of Chinese handball—the big game in his neighborhood. If you lose, you get Cans Up. You have to bend over and the winner gets to throw the ball at your butt. But this kid used a baseball instead of the soft pink rubber ball. I asked Eddie what he had done to get back at the kid and Eddie said, NOTHING.

I told him he was a wussy. You need to punish bullies right away; you need revenge, payback. Eddie said that you have to pick your spots, wait until you can get something out of all that, put points on the scoreboard. WIN. Made no sense to me, but that was Eddie. Whatever.

I didn't mind the pain because I loved the idea of having a twin brother, someone I could tell everything to, even if he *was* imaginary. I never had close friends because I changed schools a lot and because I don't like to share secrets. I don't even have too many Facebook friends, although I'm on Facebook with a phony name, so I can spy on people and hack their accounts if they're bullies.

The summer that Dad disappeared, I spent a lot of time in the backyard garden talking to Eddie. We'd have these long conversations—out loud, if I wasn't careful. Good thing I wasn't going to a psychiatrist. Imaginary twins on other planets can get you locked up in a nuthouse.

A double star double-blinked. That's the signal. We talk only at night.

Yo, Eddie. You there?

Standing on the corner.

That was a big song back in the 1950s. I Googled it first time Eddie sang it.

I think I'm going to do something bad tomorrow. It'll get me kicked out of school.

Not again, Tomaroonie.

No choice, bro. This Britzky is a bully. He has to be stopped.

Why do *you* have to stop him? You're not the Lone Ranger.

He's beating up on Alessa.

What's an Alessa?

She's, um, well, this girl . . .

You've got a friend?

Well, maybe, sort of . . .

That's super! You're cookin', good-lookin'. Now maybe there's some other way of dealing with this Bratzky.

Bratzky, I like that. Like what other way?

Talk to him. Make him your friend.

He's my enemy. I can't let him get away with what he did to Alessa.

You're not letting him get away with anything — you're looking to get something out of him, make him part of your team.

I visited Grandpa.

Changing the subject?

It was sad. He said, "The monitors have landed."

Huh. He say anything else?

He said to stay on my toes. That it was crunch time.

What's that mean?

How should I know?

The stars blinked off. That happens when he gets

called in to dinner. His grandpa is pretty strict about eating together while the food's hot.

Get Britzky on my team. Right. That's Eddie, always trying to make people his friends. Another way he was the opposite of me.

Why was I making up an opposite? What's wrong with me the way I am?

ELEVEN

DR. Traum called Eddie to his office. He tried to make Eddie feel comfortable, closing the office door, asking him to sit on the couch instead of the hard wooden chair. Dr. Traum sat on the chair himself so he could sit close to Eddie, his bright green eyes boring into him. Dr. Traum was wearing his zooty suit.

After they lost the football game, the guys on the team made fun of Dr. Traum's suit, along with the boring way he talked and how he coached. Some guys even threatened to quit the team, but Eddie met with them one at a time, face-to-face, and persuaded them to give Dr. Traum a chance. They all said they would do it for Captain Eddie.

But he's a weird one, Eddie thought. *Why am I here? Only bad kids and crazy kids go to the school psychologist.*

He would have felt better seeing Dr. Traum in the coach's office.

"This isn't coach business," said Dr. Traum.

Could he read minds?

"That was some hit you took."

"Happens all the time."

"That's what I'm worried about. Any headaches, nausea, dizziness?"

Eddie shook his head, which made him a little dizzier. The headache had almost disappeared over the weekend. *I'd better be careful,* he thought. *Any little thing could be an excuse for this guy to make me stop playing football. And then what? Basketball doesn't start for three months.*

"I hope you don't think I'm looking for an excuse to pull you off the team," said Dr. Traum. "You're a terrific quarterback. We need you."

"Thank you. I'm fine."

"I believe that, Eddie. I'm on your side. I want to prevent anything that might put you on the bench. Any flashes of light? Ringing sounds? Any changes in how your food tastes or smells? Any trouble doing homework?"

I always have trouble doing homework, thought Eddie.

"I mean, more than usual," said Dr. Traum.

Eddie's head jerked up so fast, he heard a bell ring. *Did he just read my mind?*

"These are common thoughts," said Dr. Traum. "I don't read minds."

Be careful with this guy, he is super sharp, thought Eddie. *Lying to him might be a bad idea.*

"Do you ever hear voices, Eddie?"

He stalled. "What kind of voices?"

"Maybe coming from a distance, like a radio in another room, or even inside your head. It's very common among football players."

Eddie felt super alert. He tried to read Dr. Traum as if he were reading a defense.

Dr. Traum was acting casual, like this was no big deal. Like a linebacker planning to blitz pretending he was going to drop back to defend against a pass.

"What do the voices say?"

"Different things to different people," said Dr. Traum. "They might even suggest things for you to do." He chuckled. "Try a fumble-rooski."

"A fumble what?" Eddie could tell that Dr. Traum was trying to be friendly. He relaxed a little.

"After the snap, the quarterback puts the ball . . ." Dr. Traum stopped and shook his head. "Just a little joke, Eddie. Tell me about the voices."

Eddie thought about the voice he'd been hearing for almost two years, since Dad disappeared. A kid's voice, his age. For a while, once a week; then months of silence;

then it would start again. Sometimes he thought he heard music, too—maybe a violin. At first, he thought it was Dad trying to tell him from Heaven that everything was all right. But it was a kid's voice from very far away, telling him about his life. He thought he mostly heard it after he got his bell rung, hit by a pitch, knocked down under the basket. But he'd gotten his bell rung so often, especially in football season, it was hard to know for sure.

Dr. Traum leaned back and put on a sympathetic smile. Eddie thought that maybe he could trust this guy. After all, he was the school psychologist, too.

"I hear this voice sometimes . . ."

"Your father?" Dr. Traum leaned forward, his eyes glittering.

"No. A kid. He says his name is Tom and that he's my twin brother."

Dr. Traum seemed a little disappointed, but he nodded, as if he had heard of such things before. "Where is this, um, Tom?"

"On another planet. Am I crazy?"

"Of course not. I hear this all the time. Very common. Especially among football players. Do you ever hear from your dad?"

"He disappeared," said Eddie. "Everybody says he's dead."

"What do you think?"

Eddie was beginning to feel uncomfortable. He shrugged.

"That's enough for now, Eddie. You've been a good boy. I know it's unusual for the school psychologist to also be the football coach, but that will give us a chance to know each other better. I'm going to recommend to the coach"—Dr. Traum laughed and winked—"that you take a day or two off from contact drills. But you can keep practicing, and you can start the next game." He stood up and extended his hand. "We'll talk again."

Eddie stood up and shook hands. Dr. Traum's was cold. Now his green eyes were cold, too. But he was smiling. Eddie wondered if he had made a mistake telling him about Tom.

Out in the hall, he almost bumped into Merlyn, the new cheerleader.

"Eddie! I've been looking for you." She had green eyes, too, but her hand on his arm was warm. "We're collecting canned food for starving children in Africa. I'm the girl leader, and it would be great if you were the boy leader."

"I've got football every day and . . ."

"It won't take too much time. The principal said we can get out of classes to do it. We have to think of the whole planet, not just us. Please say yes. Please."

"Yes."

Her silvery voice rose. "Hooray for Eddie!" She ran down the hall, her long black hair whipping from side to side.

TWELVE

I SET off a simple stink bomb, my specialty. You can get the recipe online and the ingredients at home. This one had enough of a rotten-egg smell to chase the class out of the room. That part is easy. The trick is in the blast. The explosion has to mostly stay in the box so no one gets burned, but there has to be enough outward force to make something happen—in this case, blow open Britzky's desk drawer.

I decided to do it in homeroom, where we all have assigned desks. It was easy enough to get to school early on my bike and open the homeroom door and then Britzky's locked desk with a TPT SafecrackerPlus. I'd assembled the bomb at home, so all I had to do was hook it up.

It was one of my best. Right after the Pledge of Allegiance, Britzky touched the knob on his drawer—BANG!—and the drawer shot open and a green cloud rose right into his face. He started gagging and coughing and crying.

The stench rose as the green cloud broke up and spread around the room. Kids who had started to laugh covered their noses and ran out.

I was glad to see no one was shooting this.

But I just sat there, grinning, as Britzky slowly got up and the teacher looked my way.

Maybe I wanted to get caught.

THIRTEEN

I AM disappointed," said Dr. Traum. That word again. "What would you do if you were in my shoes?"

I looked under his desk. He was wearing his usual laceless sneakers. "I'd change them."

He didn't react. "How is your mother going to feel? She begged me to admit you." When I didn't say anything, he sighed. "You didn't mean to hurt him, did you, Thomas?"

Good question. I hadn't thought about it. Just when I started thinking about it, a school secretary came into the office and said, "His mother's out of town, and the man who answered said he's too busy right now."

"Too busy?" Dr. Traum stood up so fast his chair rolled back into the wall and bounced forward into his legs. "Tell him he can pick up Thomas here or at the police station."

When the secretary left, Dr. Traum looked down at me. "You know, Thomas, I bent the rules to admit you." He sat down and tapped his keyboard. He squinted at his screen. "I've never seen a seventh-grader with so many past, um, incidents. False fire alarms. Bathroom floodings. Why do you think you keep getting chances?"

I knew he was going to tell me.

"These test scores. So high in math *and* reading. Musical talent. Everybody thinks a boy like you can be as terrific as he should be. And we all want to help. You understand what I'm saying?"

"I saw the movie."

He smiled. "That's what I mean, Thomas. You're way ahead of your age—quick, sharp . . . and ready to turn the corner? What do you say? A new start. I'm going to discuss this with the principal. A short suspension, some time in special ed. What do you say?"

"Special Ed's okay, but I like his brother Driver Ed better."

Dr. Traum clapped his hands. "So we have a deal? No more incidents. Turn the corner. Be as terrific as you should be."

"How terrific is that?"

"That's up to you, isn't it? Be an honor roll student, win violin competitions, make friends . . ." He paused. "Besides Eddie, of course."

The door opened and the secretary said, "Someone will be here in ten minutes."

Dr. Traum was still smiling. "What'll it be, Thomas? Deal or no deal?"

"No deal," I said.

I couldn't wait to get out of there. *Besides Eddie?* Who could have told him about Eddie? Who knew about Eddie, besides me?

FOURTEEN

THE Lump didn't say a word until we were halfway home. "This is it for you, pal. Next stop, military school."

"Cool. I want to learn how to shoot automatic weapons."

"More likely a juvenile facility full of Bronx gangbangers."

"Better," I said. "I want to learn how to kill with my bare hands."

He laughed through his fat nose, a sound like a toilet flushing. "How long do you think a skinny twelve-year-old smackmouth is going to last in a juvie zoo?"

"Long enough to come back and smoke you while you sleep."

"I feel sorry for you, Tom. You don't have to be such a loser, but you can't keep your mouth shut."

To prove him wrong, I kept my mouth shut the rest of the way home. Maybe that was what he wanted.

FIFTEEN

THE Lump and I don't eat together when Mom's out of town. I stayed up in my room all morning, searching for new apps, while he banged around the kitchen, opening and closing cabinets, the refrigerator, the microwave. I could hear him chewing and swallowing. It sounded like a garbage disposal.

And then he was blasting the big plasma TV in the living room, watching ESPN in the middle of the day. One of the reasons Mom bought it was so she and I could watch old movies together, but the Lump took it over for sports. I never watch sports.

I had a headache. First, I felt like I got hit on the back of my head; then my eyes crossed, and everything went dark for a moment. Now I just had a dull ache. I wondered if something had happened to Eddie.

I'd stayed cool when Dr. Traum mentioned Eddie and

didn't think about it while I was with the Lump, but sitting in front of my computer in my room, I let two opposite feelings wash over me. One feeling wanted to freak out—how did he know about Eddie? Was he a mind reader? I never mentioned Eddie to anybody. The other feeling was a kind of relief. I couldn't be completely insane if he knew about Eddie and hadn't thrown me into a loony bin.

I forced myself to concentrate on something else. I Googled juvenile facilities. The website of the nearest one said it was "secure." Some fourteen-year-old kid who shot a cop was there, waiting for his trial. Would I be sent to a "secure" facility or one you could escape from? If I escaped, where would I go? This is the kind of thing I could discuss only with Eddie.

I read more about the secure juvenile facility. It was thirty miles from my house. Years ago it had been a mental asylum called the Union County Hospital for the Criminally Insane. In the picture, it looked almost like a castle, with gray stone towers and tiny barred windows. It was surrounded by a high chainlink fence topped with barbed wire. Outside the fence was a stone guardhouse, where cars were inspected before they were allowed through the gate.

People had called the insane asylum a "snake pit" because inmates were locked away in little cells and treated badly—sometimes even beaten and starved. Not everybody there was a criminal. Patients who were released complained about the awful conditions and the constant noise of inmates screaming and banging their tin cups against the bars, but nothing happened until 1957, when a tornado hit the asylum and some of the patients escaped through a secret tunnel between the main building and the guardhouse.

They told reporters that it hadn't been a tornado, it had been a spaceship with aliens. But no one believed them because they were . . . well, patients in an insane asylum.

It was a big story back then because tornadoes were rare in that part of New Jersey. This one just knocked off that one tower and did no other damage anywhere. In any case, there was an investigation, and the asylum was closed for a while before it became a juvenile prison. I wondered if Eddie had heard about it back in 1957.

I took a nap and when I woke up, it was evening. I heard the basement door slam. The Lump was finally heading back down to his temperature-controlled, bomb-proof safe room. It's filled with computer equipment. He says he works for the government. When I ask him which government, he flashes his yellow werewolf teeth at me.

As usual, there were dirty dishes and glasses on the

kitchen table and in the sink. What a pig. He had eaten most of the chicken Mom had left for both of us. What was left had his teeth marks on it.

I had a peanut butter and mustard sandwich on an English muffin and a glass of milk.

I went out into the yard.

I waited a long time for the double-blink.

Where've you been, Eddie?

At Heartbreak Hotel.

That was an Elvis Presley song. Eddie loved Elvis.

I'm suspended. Going to be expelled again.

What for?

I blew up Bratzky with a stink bomb.

That was dumb. What did you get out of that?

You kidding? You should have seen the look on his face.

But you're gone and he's still there. Who's going to protect your girlfriend now?

So what do you hear from your head?

How'd you know I got dinged in the game?

I felt it. Maybe you have a concussion.

Nah, happens all the time. I had to talk to the school psychologist. He wanted to know if I heard voices.

What did you say?

I told him about you. Everything's okay. He said it happens a lot to football players. He should know. Dr. Traum's also the coach.

Wait a minute — what's his name?

Gotta pack for Scout camp. Later, alligator.

The star blinked off.

Eddie, come back. I need to talk to you.

I stood in the dark feeling stupid. It's really pathetic when you can't even have a conversation with your imaginary twin brother. The reason you make up somebody is so he's there when you need him.

Dr. Traum?

Maybe I really am insane.

SIXTEEN

NEARMONT, N.J.
1957

AFTER the new psychologist sent for him, Ronnie thought about ditching school. Couldn't be good. What did the headshrinker want? The last one had been on his case forever about where he was living. No one ever answered the telephone at the foster home listed in his records because no one was ever there. The phone was at a summer house on the lake that was shut down for the season. The people who lived there were in the city. Ronnie had thought he wouldn't have to worry until next summer. He thought he had them all faked out. Unless this new shrink got nosy.

Why can't they leave me alone? I don't need anybody to take care of me. I'm doing just fine living on my own.

Ronnie decided he'd better go see the guy. Eddie had said Dr. Traum seemed okay. But Eddie was too trusting. Teachers and psychologists act like they're your friends, and then they call the social workers or the police. *I don't want to spend another weekend at the Union County Hospital for the Criminally Insane just because they don't have any other place to put me. I was lucky they didn't give me a physical exam there. Or make me shower while someone watched.*

"Ronnie Roman." Dr. Traum waved him into his office and pointed to a hard wooden chair. He had a folder in his hand. He was a little strange looking. Bright green eyes, shiny skin. He wore a pale green zoot suit with huge lapels. Strange for someone in school.

Stay sharp, Ronnie told himself.

Dr. Traum opened the folder. "You've been in foster care for eight years. Must be difficult." He was trying to sound sympathetic. What a phony.

"It's okay."

"My predecessor in this position"—Dr. Traum waved the folder—"suggested a full-scale investigation into your situation."

Ronnie felt like taking it on the lam. Bust out of the office. Jump on a freight train, head west.

"You don't have to run away, Ronnie. I have a different plan. I know you and Eddie Tudor are good friends, and I'm worried about Eddie."

"What's wrong?" Ronnie felt a hand squeezing his heart. Eddie was the best.

"He took a hard hit in the last game. You know Eddie —too loyal to the team to admit he could be hurt. I need someone to keep an eye on him, let me know if something seems amiss."

"Like what?" Ronnie wondered if he could trust this guy. Probably not. But he could pretend.

"Dizziness, a change in how he acts. He might hear voices in his head. I'd especially want to know about that."

"What would you do?"

Dr. Traum smiled. "I can tell you are a good friend, and that makes me comfortable entrusting you with this. In cases like this, a person might think he's hearing from a loved one who died."

"His father?"

"Exactly. If that happens, I'd want to talk to Eddie some more, make sure he doesn't get hit again, which could be very dangerous." Dr. Traum stood up. "You do this for Eddie and I'll make sure nobody delves too deeply into your situation. Understand? Is that a deal?"

"You better believe it." Ronnie slipped off the chair. He shook Dr. Traum's outstretched hand, which fishy cold.

Ronnie wasn't sure it was a deal, but the cre him by the throat. *Nobody delves too deeply i situation.* Did Dr. Traum know? Ronnie wonder should tell Eddie the truth. Captain Eddie could take it, maybe even have some good ideas. But Eddie-O had enough on his mind.

What if something's wrong with Eddie? The hand on his heart tightened. Eddie was the reason he was still in school. Eddie took care of him. Maybe he could help take care of Eddie.

SEVENTEEN

T HE Lump was supposed to drive me to my violin lesson that evening. I waited by his car with my violin backpack until it was too late to go. I should have banged on his basement door, but I couldn't make myself ask him for anything. So I texted my violin teacher that I was sick. I felt so sorry for myself at missing the lesson and angry at the Lump for making me feel sorry that I just started walking down our street to the county road. I didn't know what I was going to do until I saw the bus to the city and climbed aboard.

No matter what time of day or night it is, when bus drivers and cops see my padded violin backpack, they figure I'm going to or coming from a lesson. They never hassle me, never check to see if I'm a runaway.

It took about an hour to get to midtown Manhattan. The cell phone in my sock kept vibrating, but I didn't pull it out. It was Mom calling and texting from Chicago or Dallas or wherever her company had sent her this week to take doctors out to dinner so they would prescribe the new pill that cures people of feeling shy at parties.

By now, the Lump had told her what happened at school. She'd be upset.

Hey, Mom, that's what you get for not being around.

I rode the subway down to Union Square and watched the skaters for a while. Most of them weren't too good—they were posers—but I liked their rebel cool. At least they weren't zombies.

From there, I walked down to Washington Square Park in the Village. I felt a little crabby, so I blew off steam by mime-walking, which I think I invented. You get behind somebody and imitate the way they walk. You waddle or lurch or skip. My favorite is to get behind some musclehead and swagger like I'm king of the sidewalk. People always laugh at that one. You have to be ready to run in case the musclehead turns around. I also do junkies and fat ladies, which some people don't think is funny.

Eddie thinks mime-walking is *cruel*. He doesn't believe in making fun of people, even if they deserve it. I imagine that people like him but aren't afraid of him.

That's why he's my opposite. I'd much rather people were afraid of me than like me.

Because of mime-walking and thinking about Eddie, I let my guard down. I was in the Village before I sensed that I was being followed. It was just a feeling at first, but then the hairs on the back of my head got itchy. I stopped in front of store windows to catch the reflections behind me. I made four left turns in a row. I made sudden stops, pretending to tie my shoe or check my phone. I had learned all that when I hacked into a police academy website. Nothing. But the feeling got stronger.

It was a nice night and the park was crowded with college students, who are mostly zombies. The hustlers, dope dealers, and muggers who prey on them are werewolves and vampires. That's what Dad called them. *Sometime I'll talk to Alessa about that*. She would understand. Dad was into that stuff way before all those dumb books and movies and games.

Dad told me that most people are zombies, sleepwalking through life, pushed along by the crowd, doing what they're told. Werewolves are stupid, he said, but dangerous because they're strong and can rip people apart. Thugs and most jocks are werewolves. A lot of people want to be vampires because they think vampires are sexy and have power, but they are mostly showoffs who fool other people, like actors and politicians and everybody on TV.

Dad said to remember that zombies, werewolves, and vampires don't exist but that knowing about them was a good way of figuring out how real people were going to act.

Dad said the most important thing was to hold on to being human. He never got to tell me what he meant.

I felt eyes scraping at me in the park. I imagined werewolves thinking, *Who is this skinny kid with the violin backpack? Does he have something we want?*

I thought, *You feel lucky, punk? Try and get it.* I patted the Tech9 Screamer in its shoulder holster and the cell phone bombs in my pockets. *I'm ready. Are you?*

EIGHTEEN

I GOT bumped from behind on my right side. I'd trained myself after hacking into an army commando site to respond to unexpected attacks. I spun left, crouched, got my hands out.

A girl's familiar voice said, "I'm a Russian Commie—don't kill me." She was laughing at me. She had a sweet, silvery laugh. She was pulling a rolling suitcase. She was around my age. Long dark hair covered most of her face.

It was the girl from Mrs. Rupp's class.

"Merlyn?"

She pointed at my violin backpack. "Are you here to play?"

I hadn't thought of it. "Maybe," I said.

"You want to work together? We can split what we make."

"What do you play?"

"Magic," she said.

We sat down on the rounded edge of the fountain. She opened her suitcase and took out a folding table, a collapsible top hat, and four red balls. Then she laid the opened suitcase in front of the table.

I took out my violin, tuned it, and warmed up with my side of the dueling violins from *Riverdance,* which made Merlyn smile. Then I played "Lucy in the Sky with Diamonds," one of Dad's favorites. We used to play it for Mom. She loved the Beatles. She stopped listening to her Beatles discs when the Lump moved in. He hates the Beatles. Once I heard Metallica coming through his safe-room door. Dad hated heavy metal, so I do, too. We were getting into rap when he disappeared.

A crowd was forming in front of us. I looked it over. Mostly college kids, tourists, and hustlers. Two big guys stood out, both of them dressed in white uniforms, like paramedics. Muscleheads. They had crewcuts. They seemed to be staring at me and edging closer.

Merlyn whispered, "Keep playing." In a loud voice, she said, "Welcome, folks, to the Tom and Merlyn Show. He does magic with his violin, and I fiddle with your minds."

She pulled a red scarf out of the top hat and pretended to push it into one of my ears. I kept playing.

Then she reached around my head and pretended to pull a red scarf out of my other ear. A good trick.

"Just as I thought," she said. "Tom's head is empty."

The crowd laughed—well, everybody was laughing except the two muscleheads. I could feel their stares.

Merlyn pulled a white toy bird out of the hat and put it on top of my head. I kept playing. I went right into "A Hard Day's Night." Some people started singing. Then they started laughing again as something began trickling down my face. Was the bird pooping on my head? It was confetti. Merlyn scooped it up and threw it into the crowd.

People liked us. They threw coins and dollar bills into Merlyn's open suitcase.

I played "All Together Now" and "Strawberry Fields Forever" while she did card tricks and had people come up so she could pull coins and Ping-Pong balls out of their ears. I kept peeking at her out of the corner of my eye. She was really good. She could be a professional.

Suddenly, she said, "I gotta go, Tom." She was throwing everything into her suitcase, and then she was gone. What was her hurry?

I was enjoying myself, but it was getting late. I put my violin into its backpack and slipped the straps over my shoulders. At school tomorrow I'd ask Merlyn why she split so fast. And collect my share of the money.

I was almost out of the park when I felt shoulders pressing on each side of me, steering me along. It was the two guys in white squeezing me between them.

"Just keep walking natural, and you won't get hurt," one of them said.

"Okay," I said. I made my voice small and squeaky. "Please don't kill me."

"I won't," he said, laughing. "But Earl might."

The other one just grunted.

They relaxed. They thought they had the skinny dork. As soon as I felt the pressure from their shoulders let up, I dropped into a squat and pulled the Tech9 Screamer out of its shoulder holster. I tapped the button. The Screamer was set for the max on Siren2, which sounds like a cop car coming straight at you.

When they looked around, I jumped free and headed out of the park.

But not fast enough. The one called Earl caught up to me. He grabbed my shoulder. I couldn't break free, but I wriggled loose enough to pull out a cell phone bomb. I pretended to take his picture.

He panicked and lunged at me. "Gimme that."

Last thing werewolves want is for you to have their picture.

I tossed him the cell phone and ran as fast as I could,

which wasn't fast enough because I kept looking around. I wanted to see his expression when the pepper-spray packet in the phone exploded in his face. I hadn't used one in combat before. But I missed it because I ran right into a blue wall. A cop.

NINETEEN

WHEN the sergeant behind the desk in the precinct house said, "Your ride's here, kid," my stomach twisted. I knew who was here.

The Lump walked in with a cop who had gold braid on his cap. "I appreciate this, chief. Owe you one."

"We're on the same team." The chief shook the Lump's hand.

The Lump grabbed my arm and steered me out of the precinct and into his car. Once we were on a highway heading out of the city, he said, "The cops said you were running away from something. What was it?"

"So what's this 'We're on the same team' stuff?"

"Classified," he said. "What happened in the park?"

"Classified," I said.

We didn't talk for the rest of the ride.

It was way after midnight when we got home. Mom

was waiting outside the house, pacing in the driveway. Her suitcase was on the steps. She pulled me out of the car and hugged me.

When the Lump got out, Mom hugged him and said, "Thanks, Keith."

I said, "Don't thank him. If he had taken me to my lesson, none of this would have happened."

Lump shrugged. "Noted."

Like he cared.

"What did happen?" said Mom.

"I got picked up by the cops for WWU."

"For what?"

"Walking while underage."

She nodded. "That's what Keith texted me."

"So then you know it has to be true," I said as sarcastically as possible.

"I guess so," said Mom.

Keith just gave me his yellow-fang smile.

TWENTY

As much as I hated to eat with the Lump, I stuck around while his big mouth vacuumed up most of the Chinese food Mom had ordered in. I wanted to hear what he had to say.

Rice dribbled out as he talked. "We need to finish our conversation, Denise."

It sounded like he wanted me to leave, so I grabbed a couple of dumplings, leaned back in my chair, and ate them very, very slowly.

"What conversation?" said Mom.

"You know," he said.

"I guess I don't." Mom sounded annoyed. I liked that.

The Lump said, "Tom, would you excuse us?"

"I might excuse Mom, not you."

I liked when his face got red as his whiskers.

"Denise, could you get me a beer?"

I hated it when that lumpy Lump ordered Mom around. I jumped up. "I'll get it."

I opened the refrigerator door and angled it so they couldn't see me shake the beer bottle a couple of times. Hard.

"Here." I banged it down in front of the Lump. If I acted too nice, he'd get suspicious.

He didn't even say thanks as he twisted open the top.

FSSSST! an explosion of foam, all over him.

While he was yelling and jumping around, I stuck a TPT FloatingEar wireless remote mike to the underside of the table.

I grabbed a couple more dumplings and excused myself.

I got up to my room and pulled on the headset in time to hear him say, "You'll be sorry if he hurts somebody. Or himself."

Mom was sniffling. "He's going through a phase, Keith."

"He needs a major workup."

"A what?"

"Brain scans, chemical analysis, neural tracking."

"He's twelve years old, Keith. If I don't know him by now . . ."

"But you don't really know him—that's my point.

You don't really know that much about his dad, and you know nothing about his biological mother."

Biological mother? I jumped up. I had to put a hand over my mouth.

"Who told you that?" snapped Mom.

The Lump said, "I figured it out."

"How?"

"Everything's out there if you know where to look," he said.

There was a long pause. I could hear the Lump chewing and Mom breathing hard. I was breathing hard, too. *Mom?* She was still Mom, but . . .

Finally, Mom said, "That's enough. Let's see what happens."

"You need to do something before it's too late."

"What does that mean?" She sounded angry.

"It means something's going on with him. He's out of control. You ever hear him talking to himself in the backyard?"

"You eavesdrop on him?"

"Not like he eavesdrops on us." There was static and a thump. "Look at this."

"What's that?"

He'd found my transmitter under the table. "It could have been a bomb."

Crunch, and then silence.

TWENTY-ONE

MOM waited while I brushed my teeth, and then she tucked me in as if I were a little kid. I liked it and I hated it. She sat on the edge of the bed and hugged me. "Are you okay, Tommy?"

"Yeah."

She held me tight. "What are we going to do with you?"

"Send me to military school."

"Where'd you get that idea?"

"The Lump."

"I really wish you wouldn't call him that."

"How about Pigmeat?"

She took a deep breath. "With your grandfather in a nursing home," she said, "we need the rent Keith pays. And I feel better with a man in the house, especially when I travel."

"I hate him," I said.

"Please, Tom." She put her face so close to mine I could feel the tears on her eyelashes. "I can't go on like this."

"Like what?"

"I had to leave the conference, fly home. I'm going to lose my job if it happens again."

"Some job. Selling pills so people can get dates."

She leaned away from me. "Who told you that?"

"Dad."

"He never said that."

"He did. Just before he disappeared, he said it was sad that you quit being a nurse to peddle pills."

"He never understood," said Mom. She looked both sad and angry. "He was never around. God knows what he did."

"You don't know what he did?"

She shrugged. "A private man, your dad."

"He was a great dad."

"When he was around, he was a great dad. And a great husband," she said. "I always thought he had another life, a secret life."

"Like a superhero?"

Mom smiled. Sometimes I forgot how pretty she was. "Could be. He was very strong. And so smart. Like you. And he hated bullies."

She looked dreamy. She was off-guard. So I jumped in with the question I'd been waiting to ask. "What about my biological mother?"

She jerked back as if I'd hit her. "What are you talking about?"

"I heard what the Lump said." When she opened her mouth, I said, "Tell me the truth."

Her mouth snapped shut. She blinked a couple of times. Finally, she took another deep breath and nodded. "Your birth mother died when you were born."

"Why didn't you tell me?"

"Your father made me promise. He said he wanted to do it himself when the time was right."

"When was that going to be?" I made my face very hard so I wouldn't cry.

She was crying. "He was getting ready to tell you when he died."

"Disappeared."

"All I can tell you, Tommy, is I've loved you as much as if you had come out of my body." She reached out to hug me.

I squirmed away. "Get out!" I shouted.

"I know this is very hard for you . . ."

"You don't know anything." I jumped out of bed, pushed past her, and ran out of the house.

TWENTY-TWO

EDDIE's grandpa was silent on the ride to Scout camp, which was okay with Eddie. He felt good dozing in the front seat of the big Dodge. The radio softly played the country-western tunes Grandpa liked, "A White Sport Coat," "I Walk the Line," and "Hound Dog," Eddie's own favorite. He loved Elvis.

Eddie came fully awake when the car turned off the highway and bumped down a dirt road into the woods. It stopped at a clearing.

"Where are we, Grandpa?"

"Where we need to be." He turned and faced Eddie. He looked very serious. "You're going to have to trust me, son."

"I've always trusted you, Grandpa."

Grandpa nodded. "You're going to take a trip, Eddie. By yourself."

"To Scout camp."

"No. To another planet."

Eddie laughed. "Altair IV?"

"What?"

"*The Forbidden Planet*. The movie we saw. Remember Robby the Robot?"

Grandpa shook his head. "This is no movie, Eddie. This is real. You're going back to the planet where you were born. You're going to meet your twin brother, Tom."

Eddie just stared at him. The old man was no jokester. "Tom? My twin brother?"

"This is going to be a lot for you to take in, but try to follow me. Twelve years ago, when you and Tom were born, you were separated. For your safety. Tom stayed on EarthOne, you came here. Now it's time."

Eddie's head hurt. He was confused. "Time for what?"

"To meet each other. To switch places. To learn about each other's home planets. To get ready for the rebellion to save the Earths."

"What about football? I'm the captain."

Grandpa smiled. He reached out and ran a hand through Eddie's short hair. "*We* need captains, too. Let's go. We don't have much time."

Grandpa got out of the car. He was carrying Eddie's food sack. When Eddie went to get his duffel, his grandpa said, "You won't need that."

Eddie followed Grandpa deeper into the woods, to a clearing.

"Just stand there," said Grandpa. "Against that tree. Here." He handed Eddie the food.

"What's going to happen?" Eddie asked. He felt a little panicky. He ordered himself to swallow it down. *Hang tough. Pretend it's a game. You're waiting to get the ball.*

"You're going to feel lousy for a couple of hours. It's not easy slipping through space and time. But you'll be fine, and I'll be there to meet you and tell you what to do."

Grandpa glanced at his watch. "Here we go." He hugged Eddie harder and longer than he ever had before. When he stepped back, his eyes looked teary. "Happy trails, son."

He took a small black box out of his pocket and adjusted the dials. He pressed a button.

Eddie felt himself slipping away.

TWENTY-THREE

Eddie? You there?

He'd always been there for me before. Sometimes weeks would go by without us talking, but when I called, he'd show up.

One time I Googled "imaginary friends" and read about how they were normal and even helped some kids learn to think and speak. But then I read stuff that said imaginary friends could be a sign of being off your rocker.

I'd been to doctors a few times about my behavior at school. They told Mom I was "acting out" because I was missing Dad and that when I understood that he was dead and not just disappeared, I would get better.

Eddie? I really need to talk to you.

Sometimes the doctors prescribed pills for me. I got good at cheeking them, even when Mom or nurses were watching. A couple of times I even spat them into the Lump's beer and watched him drink it. The pills never seemed to affect him.

Right now I was feeling lousy, like I was coming down with the flu.

I couldn't even find the double stars.

Eddie? She was your mom, too.

The flu was getting worse. My body ached from being squeezed on all sides. It was hard to breathe. I felt like I had to go to the bathroom even though I didn't.

I waited until all the lights were out before I went back into the house.

I couldn't sleep. My stomach felt like the inside of a washing machine. My eyeballs ached. Chills. I tried to ignore them. I played a game of Ambush III against myself. Everybody died. I got tired of the game. I couldn't concentrate. Too many questions in my head. Mom wasn't my mother. Why hadn't Dad told me? What was he waiting for? What else didn't I know about myself?

I tried to clear my mind by surfing the tech blogs. I hacked around until I found the company memos on the CloakII, which I had put together from a kit I got online. It was an invisibility machine. I never got it to work. The company was also having trouble with the CloakII. I read on a national security blog that the army was working on a machine just like it that could bend light so that soldiers would be invisible. The big problem with the machine was that it distorted the light waves for only a few seconds before you became visible again. I had worked on the CloakII off and on for almost a year.

Suddenly, I felt as though I were upside down, which made me nauseous. I thought about Eddie, and when I thought about Eddie, I felt as though I were whooshing through space.

Then I hauled out my violin and played a few bars from dueling violins before it made me too sad thinking about Dad. I played solos from *The Lord of the Rings* songbook Grandpa gave me a few years ago, "Into the West" and "Gollum's Song." They really need a piano accompaniment, but Grandpa can't read music anymore and Mom's the only other piano player I know. She's too busy.

"Sounds good." The Lump had walked into my room and sat down on my bed. "From *Rings,* right?"

"What part of knocking is too hard for you?"

"The part where you tell me to buzz off."

That's the worst, when he tries to act friendly.

I ignored him and played "Evenstar."

"I saw those flicks three times," he said. "People said I looked like Gimli."

"The dwarf?"

He nodded.

He was right. He was a big, ugly red-haired version of Gimli. "Too bad. Up until this minute, Gimli was one of my favorite characters."

"Look, Tom, your mom is very upset."

"You think?"

"For her sake, how about a truce?"

"How about you move out?"

"She doesn't want that."

"You want *me* out," I said.

"Not true. I just want to get along with you."

"Then leave me alone." I didn't want to talk to him. I turned my back on him.

After a while, I heard him get up. He said, "This is my most private number. You can always get me on it." He walked out of my room.

He'd left his card with a number written on it. I crumpled it and threw it in the wastebasket. Then I changed my mind and took it out. I might want to send him a virus text someday.

When I got into bed, my cell beeped. It was a text from Merlyn.

Come back to school tomorrow. Be cool.

Could I trust her?

TWENTY-FOUR

KIDS were surprised to see me. On the bus and in the hall, they grinned and nodded at me. Nobody liked Britzky. Sometimes I nodded back, but mostly I tried not to react. *Be cool.*

Teachers ignored me in class except for Mrs. Rupp, who shook her head at me before ignoring me for the rest of the period. I kept my mouth shut even when she started with her timeline again. I didn't see Merlyn in the class, so I couldn't find out what she was up to. Or collect the money she owed me from performing in the park.

At lunch, Alessa said, "So what happened?"

"To who?"

Big sigh.

Why are people always big-sighing me? She lifted a carrot chip out of her salad and put it in her mouth. She ate very little, and she ate it slowly and delicately, as if she wanted to chew things to death painlessly. I think fat people must do their serious eating in private.

"Don't play with me, Tom. How did you get back into school after only one day's suspension?"

"I don't know." That was true. I could tell she didn't believe me. I wondered why I wanted her to believe me. I showed her the text from Merlyn.

"You came back on this?" Her eyes were wide. "You crazy? What if she's playing you?"

"What if Dr. Traum asked her to do it?"

"Teachers don't ask . . ." Then she stopped, as if there was something she didn't want to tell me. I could sense her mind changing directions. "Maybe he needs a really good first violinist."

"I'm not that good."

"I think you are. And so does he. The first day he showed up at school, he was more interested in the violins than anything else. That was just last week."

"He's only been here a week?"

"Yeah, one day the school psychologist and the orchestra teacher both quit, and the next day he showed up and took both jobs."

"Like he knew I was coming . . ." I said. "Weird."

Alessa pushed her big moon face close and whispered, "You're right. There's something very weird about him. Like he's from another planet."

Bang! I was suddenly on the cafeteria floor. I jumped up, my fists ready. I'd been slammed down hard. But except for Alessa, no one was anywhere near me.

Everybody was watching. Alessa said, "Are you okay?"

"What happened?"

"It was like a big invisible hand knocked you down," said Alessa.

Mrs. Rupp, who was on cafeteria duty, hurried over. "What are you up to now, Tom?"

I said, "I'm up to October first, two thousand and eleven."

"Don't you dare mock me, young man," said Mrs. Rupp. She walked away.

Alessa said, "What's with you?"

"What do you mean?"

"You don't have to be nice, but can't you ever just, you know, be chill?"

"And let them think they got to me?"

She nodded at that and went back to slowly murdering carrots.

I had the feeling Alessa knew something she wasn't telling me.

The flu symptoms were gone. They had completely disappeared the moment I fell on the floor. Had something happened to Eddie? Was it over now? Why did I think that?

TWENTY-FIVE

A T orchestra, Dr. Traum didn't say anything about my coming back to school after only a one-day suspension. He must have gotten Merlyn to write that text. Why? I pretended nothing had happened. When you're inside a mystery, you have to be cool.

Dr. Traum was nice. Too nice. He asked Alessa and me to stay after practice. He handed us sheet music. "Three Beethoven duets. Look them over and pick one for the winter concert."

I looked at the sheets. They were easy. The music I was playing for my private teacher was much more advanced. I was still mad about missing my last lesson.

"They're really hard," said Alessa.

"You'll have to rehearse. Together." Dr. Traum was smiling. I thought he winked at Alessa.

On the way out, Alessa said, "Let's start rehearsing today. At my house. Uh-oh."

Britzky and his parents were coming out of the principal's office. I figured they were his parents because they were huge and ugly like him. He pointed at me. "That's him," he said to his parents. To me he said, "It's not over, Canty."

"It is for you, Bratzky." I liked saying the name Eddie had given him. Made him seem smaller.

Alessa started dragging me away. "You have a death wish, Tom." But she was smiling. I let her steer me out the door and into her mom's car. The speakers were blasting a song called "Tough Girlz," and Alessa's mom was drumming on the steering wheel. She had a crewcut, dyed blond, and she was wearing really tight clothes and lots of jewelry. She seemed happy that Alessa had a friend, but her eyes narrowed when Alessa introduced me.

"Weren't you suspended? It was on the PTO e-mail alert."

"It was a misunderstanding," I said. "Todd Britzky forgot he agreed to store my science experiment in his desk."

Alessa gave me an elbow in the ribs, but she didn't say anything.

They lived in a fancy new house across town. Alessa's

mom put out fruit and diet soda in a big sunny room with music stands. "Would you like cookies and milk, Tom?" She shot Alessa a look as if to say, Not for you.

"No thanks. This is great."

She tiptoed out as if we were already playing.

"That was such a lie about the science experiment."

"So?"

"How do you lie like that?"

"You want lessons?"

She laughed. "Did you ever hear the expression 'chip on his shoulder'?"

"Yeah."

"You've got a whole tree on *your* shoulder."

"You want to play?"

While she tuned her cello and warmed up, I noticed she didn't use her right arm very well. Her shoulders were tight, and she was mostly pushing the bow with her forearm. Bad technique. Dad was always big on getting your muscles loose so the music would just flow out of you into the strings.

"You have to relax more," I said.

"What?"

"Your shoulders are all bunched up, so you're not using your entire arm."

"That's how I play."

"You could play better."

"Why are you picking on me?" She sounded angry.

"I'm helping you."

"You could do it in a nicer way."

"Like how?"

She looked at me. "You really don't know how, do you?" She sounded sorry for me.

"Can we just play?"

It certainly wasn't like playing a duet with Dad. Alessa tried hard. She threw plenty of energy into her bow, but her left hand was sloppy, and I had to keep slowing down. It was tough. Before it was time for me to go we got through the first duet, but not always together.

TWENTY-SIX

GRANDPA was peering down at Eddie. "How do you feel?"

Lousy, he thought, but he said, "Okay." The moment he said it, he felt better. He stood up. "Where am I?"

"You're on EarthOne now."

"Where?" said Eddie.

"I told you it was a lot to take in. There are two Earths. One is about fifty years older than the other one."

"How could that be?"

"Many years ago, the scientists on another planet began an experiment. It was called the Twinning Project," said Grandpa. "They created dozens of sets of two planets around the universe, usually starting one planet fifty years before the second one. The idea was to keep track of their evolution, see what went well and what didn't, and make changes whenever necessary.

"We're not sure what happened in the case of the Earth twins — maybe we weren't paying attention — but things got out of control. Wars, famines, genocides. Then the atomic bombs in 1945 really shook us up."

"Us? Who's us, Grandpa?"

"Good catch, Eddie. I was one of the scientists. And your dad was one of the monitors sent down to keep track of the Earths."

Eddie felt a wave of excitement. "Tell me about Dad."

"Later. We have to get you to Tom's house now."

TWENTY-SEVEN

USUALLY, I conk out as soon as my head hits the pillow, no matter what's going on, but tonight I couldn't sleep. I had the feeling that something, somebody, was in my room.

I got up and turned on all the lights.

I turned all my electronic devices on and off and back on again.

I looked out the window. I looked under the bed. There was only one place left.

I guess I was a little scared of opening the closet.

"Okay," I said loudly. "My Taser's on stun. Come out and nothing will happen to you. Otherwise, you're barbecue."

My closet door opened, and someone who looked like me stepped out.

He looked like me, but he was wearing clothes I'd

never wear: a button-down blue shirt, chinos, and sand-colored desert boots. But he looked like me. He was either me or my identical twin.

Eddie?

Tom?

He walked over and stuck out his hand. I shook it. It was a real hand.

I thought I made you up.

Made me up?

He grabbed my shoulder and knee, spun me around, and dumped me on the floor.

I was lying on my back.

Why'd you do that?

To show you I'm real.

This real?

I looped my legs around his ankles and dumped him.

We started wrestling. He was stronger and quicker, but we each seemed to know what the other was about to do, and my mind worked faster than his.

Then the Lump started banging on the wall, and we stopped, flopped back on the floor, and lay there side by side, breathing hard.

You're good, Eddie.

Almost as good as you, Tom.

It's like I'm fighting myself.

We couldn't stop staring at each other.

How'd you get here?

Slip.

Slip?

"Can you talk out loud?"

"That better?"

"Yeah. What's 'slip' mean?"

"It's how we travel between the two Earths."

"What's it like?"

"You feel sick for a couple of hours. Fever, chills, aches and pains. Then you land. Hard. And then you're okay."

"I felt that. I thought I had the flu."

The Lump's voice boomed, "Turn the TV off, Tom. Go to sleep."

"Go to hell, Lump," I said, but not loud enough for him to hear.

Eddie and I started laughing so hard, we had to cover our mouths and stick our heads under the blanket.

It was great. We were up all night.

PART TWO

THE SWITCH

TWENTY-EIGHT

I TOOK Eddie's picture with my cell phone, showed it to him, then printed it and gave it to him.

Neat little camera.

We were back to talking in our heads so the Lump wouldn't hear.

It's a cell phone.

A phone?

I can listen to my tunes, see movies, play games, send a text.

What's a text?

A text is a message.

Where are the wires?

You don't need wires.

Cowabunga!

LOL.

What?

Stands for laugh out loud. Never mind.

I showed him everything in my room: the HDTV, the TiVo, the Gameboy, the xBox, and the DVD player, which I hardly use anymore. He got so interested in my laptop that we never got to the really interesting stuff, the trackers and hackers and jammers and booby traps and screamers. Or my best stuff—the TPT SafecrackerPlus and the CloakII, even though I could never get it to work.

I showed him the YouTube of me greasing the jock bully in my last school. He watched it twice, holding his hands over his mouth so the Lump wouldn't hear him laughing. Eddie had a laugh like bells ringing that made me want to laugh along with him.

Eddie and I flopped on the bed. We couldn't stop grinning at each other. It was so fun.

He pulled a pink rubber ball out of his pocket and began squeezing it. When he noticed me looking at it, he said, It builds up your hands and forearms. You should try it.

He flipped it to me.

It might be good for the violin.

I wish I could play a musical instrument.

Maybe I can teach you. You going to stay for a while?

That's the plan, man. But you're splitting.

Where?

We're switching places tonight.

In your dreams.

I'll be you, and you'll be me.

Why?

Because of the aliens.

What aliens?

The bad guys who are after us.

That's not real. I made it all up.

You're not that smart.

Smarter than some jock who never saw a laptop. You can't even play the violin. How are you going to pretend to be me?

Just give me the ball, I'll find a way. C'mon, we've got to go.

Where?

To the slipping place. We have to go now.

Who said?

Our grandpa. He explained it all to me while we were riding over here. C'mon. He said slipping only works when the sun's at a certain latitude.

Grandpa's demented.

That's not nice.

Truth hurts.

How come your truth only hurts other people?

Okay, let's go meet this grandpa.

He said you can bring your violin, but that's all.

You nuts? I need my laptop, my iPhone, my . . .

What for?

Text, get online, Google . . .

LAL. We don't have that stuff yet.

Wait just a minute. How do we even know we're really twins?

We thought about that a long time. We stared at each other. I felt as confused as Eddie looked.

And then we stopped breathing. We had gotten the same idea at the same time.

"Scar." We said it together out loud.

We pulled down our pants. His pink scar, long and raised like mine, was on his right butt cheek. We got cheek to cheek in front of my closet mirror.

We were a match.

TWENTY-NINE

NEARMONT, N.J.
2011

EDDIE and I rode double on my bike to a field behind Grandpa's nursing home. Dad told me that all this had been woods long ago.

Grandpa was waiting beside a big old tree. It was my grandpa all right. But he was standing straight. His eyes were bright.

"Both my puppies together," he said, hugging us. "I've waited for this day."

"Is it really you?" I said. "I mean, are you feeling . . ."

"I'm fine, Tom. When the monitors landed, I needed to pretend I had dementia, so I could hide out in the nursing home."

"Wait a minute." I felt angry. "You've been lying to me, too."

"Listen up, boys," said Grandpa. He kicked some branches to clear a place on the ground. He sat down.

Eddie and I squatted close to him. "This is all happening faster than we expected. We didn't have as much time as we hoped to prepare you to switch places. So. What can you tell each other? Tom?"

"Alessa's gonna like you, Eddie, because you're me, only nice," I said. "She'll pick you up for school tomorrow at eight. Britzky is the bully who wants revenge on you."

"What can you tell him, Eddie?" said Grandpa.

"You can trust Ronnie—he's my little sidekick. Be careful of Dr. Traum, he's the—"

"There's a Dr. Traum here, too," I said.

"Uh-oh." Grandpa frowned. "Be careful, both of you. This Traum is probably a monitor. They can be in two places at the same time."

"Like you," I said.

He ignored that. "You boys are going to be just fine." He stood up. "John raised you to be rebel heroes."

He handed me a paper bag and pushed me against the tree. "I got you a turkey wrap for the trip, Tom. I'll see you on EarthTwo."

He took a small black box out of his pocket. He adjusted the dials. He pressed a button.

Eddie gave me a thumbs-up.

I felt myself moving. I was coming down with the flu again. I clutched the violin bag like it was a teddy bear. Through the padded fabric, I felt my cell, the TPT SafecrackerPlus, and my CloakII. Dr. Traum still had my TPT GreaseShot IV. I missed it. You hate to go off on an adventure without your best weapon.

But I knew I could do it. I was raised to be a rebel hero.

And then I slipped away.

THIRTY

EDDIE was confused and nervous. How could he pull this off? Tom was so smart. And all those electronic gadgets. He didn't even know how to turn them on.

Tom's bike was complicated enough. The brakes were attached to the handlebars, and there were twenty-one gears. Twenty-one! He wobbled and nearly fell off before he got the hang of gently squeezing the brakes. Grandpa had his own bicycle. Eddie followed him back to Tom's house. He rode fast for an old guy, and Eddie had trouble keeping up until he picked up the rhythm of the bike and finally figured out the gears. He began to feel less nervous.

The houses in Tom's neighborhood were bigger and fancier than the houses in Eddie's neighborhood back home on EarthTwo. There were streetlights and traffic lights and many more cars, some as big as trucks. The trees were bigger and older. But the streets seemed sort of familiar, and they had some of the same names. Elm Street. Lois Lane. Knickerbocker Avenue. Tom's house reminded Eddie of his own house, but with a second floor and a garage. There were lights on upstairs and downstairs.

"Are they having a party?" Eddie asked.

"It's just Keith, and he's probably locked away in the basement," said Grandpa. "Tom's mom is out of town for her job. Just go to Tom's room, up the stairs, first on the right. Get a good night's sleep. Alessa and her mom will pick you up at eight tomorrow morning."

"I'm scared, Grandpa."

Grandpa hugged him. "If you weren't scared, you'd be nuts, Eddie. Like your brother."

"You think Tom's nuts?"

"Kinda. He's angry — about your dad disappearing, about his mom's business trips, about her tenant in the house. He just found out that your birth mom died."

"I knew that years ago."

"You seemed ready. He didn't."

"You don't think he's scared?"

"He just shows it in a different way."

"How am I going to learn all those machines?"

"They're not hard. Every idiot on EarthOne has a phone stuck to his face. Every old lady in my nursing home is texting her grandkids. They're on Facebook . . ."

"What's a facebook?" Eddie looked worried. "See? How can I make people think I'm Tom?"

"Don't worry. Just be yourself. People will believe you've turned into a different person because you're taking special pills to help you lose your bad attitude."

"They have pills like that?"

"People here on EarthOne have been gobbling them by the handful for fifty years. Tom's mom helps to sell them. They're just starting to get big on EarthTwo."

"I don't have to really take them, do I?"

"No. But you have to say you do. And here's the good part. The cover story is that these pills have side effects. They give you amnesia for a while, so you forget names, where classrooms are, songs everybody's listening to, TV shows. It's so bad, you can't even play the violin or use your computer."

"That'll be easy to prove."

Grandpa laughed. "Any problems, just come on over to the nursing home."

"You'll be with Tom, too, right? That means you'll be in two places at the same time. Like the monitors."

"That's right."

"But you were a scientist, you told me," said Eddie.

Grandpa nodded. "I'm glad you remembered. The head scientists decided that the Earths were unstable, that they could blow themselves up and wreck the universe. They wanted to destroy them. Your dad and I were part of the group that wanted to save the Earths."

"Was Dad a scientist, too?"

"Your dad was a monitor," said Grandpa. "We both became rebels against our own planet."

"And now Tom and me are rebels, too."

"We're counting on you boys." Grandpa knuckled Eddie's head. "Now go get some sleep. Tomorrow's a big day."

He handed Eddie a key to the front door, got back on his bike, and pedaled away.

THIRTY-ONE

EDDIE tiptoed up the stairs and into Tom's room. He planned to look it over carefully, but once he sat down on Tom's bed, he decided he needed to stretch out for a few minutes first. That was it. As usual, whenever he was worried, he fell right to sleep.

He awoke early. Tom's house was noisier than his, alarms and machines humming and clicking. Because it was a big old house, it made creaky, grinding sounds. The groaning of the refrigerator downstairs almost drowned out Keith's snoring in the bedroom across the hall.

Eddie had slept in the chinos and blue shirt he was wearing when he left EarthTwo. They were wrinkled and a little stinky, but he kept them on because he felt shy about wearing Tom's clothes, which were mostly T-shirts with pictures and words on them and denim pants that looked more stylish than the dungarees he wore back home. He wasn't allowed to wear dungarees to school.

The kitchen was huge, like the kitchen in a restaurant, shiny metal and polished wood. He opened the refrigerator. It looked like a grocery store back home: boxes of berries, a cooked chicken in a plastic box, different kinds of milk and yogurt, bags of lettuce. There was a bag of green leaves marked "baby arugula." What was that? Soda, beer, soy milk. What was soy milk? Were there soy cows?

In the freezer there were various brands and flavors of ice cream, even cones and pops. Pizzas, Chinese food, and boxes of entire dinners, including meat, potatoes, and vegetables. One of them said you could microwave it in seven minutes.

I have to find out what microwave is.

Grandpa usually made him scrambled eggs, bacon, and toast for breakfast, with hot chocolate in the wintertime. Eddie didn't want to start cooking in this kitchen. He peeked into a lot of cabinets before he found the cold cereals—at least six different kinds, including organic wheat with pecan flakes. He settled for Wheaties—the Breakfast of Champions—which he had eaten at home. He put berries and one percent milk on the cereal. One percent of what? He wondered what Tom ate for breakfast.

At eight o'clock he heard a honk. There was a huge black car, more like a delivery van or a small truck, in the driveway. He went outside. The passenger window rolled down and a big black face smiled at him. "Hey, Tom. You look soooo preppy."

It had to be Alessa, but Eddie was surprised. Tom had never said she was colored. There weren't any Negroes in Eddie's school. Not that they were segregated, like in the South, but no Negroes lived in the neighborhood.

Tom's best friend at school is a Negro girl, he thought, *and now she's supposed to be my best friend.* It made him nervous. What would he say to her? He didn't talk to girls that much. And he had never spoken to a Negro person.

"Let's go, Tom, we'll be late."

He opened a back door and climbed in.

The driver said, "You look very nice, Tom." She was a Negro, too, but thin. She wore a suit over a white blouse. She had very short blond hair and piles of makeup. Really pretty. Must be Alessa's older sister, a high school girl or maybe college.

"Thank you. You look very nice. Do you go to school here, too?"

She made a hooting sound. "Ohh, I think I love you, Tom."

Alessa said, "I think some alien must have taken him over, Mom."

Alien? Mom? Eddie looked back and forth between them, but they were just laughing. It didn't seem as if Alessa knew anything.

School was less than a mile away. They could have ridden bikes there—even walked, he thought. It was a red brick box, pretty much like his school but older-looking. The bricks were chipped and grimier. There was a big stone fountain out front, just like at his school.

There was a line of cars outside, most of them trucks like the one he was in. Kids were climbing out with suitcases. Some of them had wheels. Some kids had them strapped on their backs like the packs Scouts carried on overnight trips. Everybody had those little phones in their hands, and most of the kids were fiddling with them using only their thumbs. There were other Negro kids and lots of Oriental-looking kids, which was surprising, too. He wondered if he would be able to get along with them. On his planet, they'd been fighting wars with Japanese, Koreans, and even Chinese until not long ago.

When the big car pulled up to the entrance, Alessa's mom said, "Have a good one, guys." She kissed the top of Alessa's head and waved her fingers at Eddie. She had a ring on every finger.

"Thanks for the ride," he said. She gave him a big smile, and as he got out, she started talking. He turned back to answer, but she was talking to a little microphone above her head.

Alessa was waiting for him on the sidewalk outside the school. Kids rushed by. "You never got back to me."

"About what?"

"The plans for today."

"What plans?"

She scowled at him. "Well, you just check your texts. It's all there."

Texts. He remembered they were messages you get on your phone. "I don't have a phone."

"Did you leave it at home?"

Eddie remembered that he hadn't seen the little phone in Tom's bedroom. Had Tom sneaked it along?

"I've got to stop using it for a while."

"How can you do that?"

"The pills I'm taking."

"What pills?"

"I had to take these pills to change my attitude." He hated to lie, but he was surprised at how easy it was. "And they have these side effects. I can't play the violin. And I don't remember things."

"Oh, Tom, that's terrible." She squeezed his arm. "I'll help you all I can."

"Look who's here, all dressed up." A huge kid with a splash of pimples on his forehead made a big deal of looking Eddie up and down but without getting too close. "You running for class president?" He had a snorty laugh, through his nose.

A bully, thought Eddie, *but he seems scared of me. Of Tom.* He dimly remembered Tom telling him about some guy he had to stop. Bratzky?

"Fall back, pizza face," growled Alessa.

Eddie said, "Never make fun of how a person looks, Alessa. He can't help it."

That got the kid really angry. He raised his fists and Eddie got ready to duck, but a teacher suddenly appeared. "Better hurry up—bell's going to ring." She checked Eddie up and down. "You look like you had a makeover, Tom."

It took him a moment to figure out what she meant. Like he had been made over—gussied up, as Grandpa would say. The teacher seemed to be waiting for him to say something, so Eddie said the first thing that popped into his head. "I'm running for class president."

THIRTY-TWO

TOM's school was different from his in ways that made Eddie blink. He couldn't believe the way teachers dressed here on EarthOne. They dressed worse than *kids* dressed on EarthTwo! In his school, teachers wore suits and ties or dresses. Here the men teachers wore polo shirts and dungarees, and so did some of the women. The kids were all in T-shirts and dungarees, and some of the dungarees were pretty weird, with rips and colored stitches and even glass beads. And they were tight, not like the baggy dungarees on EarthTwo. Some kids had rings in their noses and lips and eyebrows. That made Eddie wince.

Right under the flag in the front of the classroom, where the picture of the president usually goes, was a photo of a Negro man. Who could that be?

Kids weren't as respectful here, but the teachers

didn't seem to mind. Everybody was jokier. Some kids and teachers greeted each other by slapping palms or bumping fists. It was weird. Nobody slapped Eddie's palm or bumped his fist, which was just as well, since he wasn't sure how to do it. They steered clear of him, didn't look him in the eye. It seemed as if most kids and teachers didn't like him. Or were afraid of him. Eddie felt sorry for Tom.

And for myself, Eddie thought. *I'm a friendly guy, and hanging out with other kids is the best part of school. That's why teams are so great. This is really lonely.*

Alessa was in all his classes, so he just followed her from room to room, and she pointed him to Tom's seat. The teachers didn't call on him. A good thing, he thought. Math was hard. Forget French. In his school only the eggheads took French. Eddie was taking Spanish.

At lunch, Alessa said, "I loooved the way you put Britzky down. 'Never make fun of how a person looks.'"

Britzky, the kid she had called pizza face, was glaring at them from across the cafeteria.

"I meant it," Eddie said.

"Sure you did."

The cafeteria was a pretty neat place. There was a long serving counter with all kinds of hot meals, cheeseburgers, food with Spanish names, salads, different sizes and shapes of spaghetti, a dozen different sodas. Each thing had its own little sign, with its name and the number of calories in it. Eddie knew what calories were, but he had never worried about them. He needed to eat a lot to keep his weight up, especially during football season. When he asked Alessa about the school's football team and she said the team was disbanded last year because there wasn't enough interest, he felt let down.

Eddie got something called a wrap with turkey and cheese inside. He remembered that Grandpa had given Tom a wrap for the slip trip. Back home, most kids brought their own sandwiches to school. Grandpa always packed Eddie monster sandwiches — roast beef, chicken, meat loaf — enough to share with Ronnie. Eddie would buy containers of milk and cupcakes for both of them.

He followed Alessa to a table at the far corner of the cafeteria near the garbage barrels, which was interesting, because he could see what was going on at all the other tables. Back home, he sat with the team that was in season — football in fall, basketball in winter, and baseball in spring — usually in the middle of the cafeteria near the social kids and the politicians. The other kids watched *them*.

At Alessa's table, Eddie was the only one wearing a shirt with a collar except for one freaky-looking boy who was wearing a black tuxedo and a black bow tie. He had black makeup around his eyes, which made him look like a raccoon. Eddie figured he was in a school play. Back home, he'd better be in a school play or he'd get beaten up for looking like that.

Actually, most of the kids at his table would have gotten run out of his junior high school. There was a girl with green hair and a boy whose head was shaved except for the hairy letters RU1? on both sides. And their clothes were like costumes: funny plaids, torn pants, pants hanging real low. Back home, everybody dressed pretty much the same—skirts and blouses for the girls, chinos and checked shirts or blue button-downs for the boys.

"This is kooky," whispered Eddie.

Alessa nodded and sighed. She sighed a lot for a kid. Maybe she had trouble breathing. "I feel like we're living in a reality show."

He almost had to bite his tongue so he wouldn't ask her what a reality show was. Maybe a reality show was like a variety show. Like the *Ed Sullivan Show.*

Britzky, the kid with the bad forehead, was sitting at a table of jocks—but at the end, like he was the last man on the bench. Eddie had that on his Earth, too, where the worst jock bully was usually a guy who barely made the team, a guy who needed to show off so he could feel like part of the group. *Keep that in mind when you deal with Britzky,* he told himself.

"You really going to run for president, Tom?" asked the girl with green hair.

Eddie shrugged. His mouth was full of the wrapped turkey and cheese, which he liked.

"Better lose those preppy duds," said the kid with eye makeup. He was pointing at Eddie.

"Preppy's back," said Alessa. "It'll be a new look for a new Tom. A leader, not a troublemaker."

"We need troublemakers," said the green-haired girl. "Don't you think, Tom?"

Eddie had no idea what to say, so he said, "I really like your hair." Lying was getting so easy, he thought.

"Green is for the environment," she said. "If we don't stand up for the environment, the corporations are going to wreck it, just to make money."

"I agree," said Eddie. He wasn't sure what she meant, but he wanted to start making friends. "We have to think of the whole planet, not just us." Where had he heard that? Merlyn. The canned-goods drive for starving kids.

There was a sudden silence at the table, and then everyone was smiling and trying to fist-bump him and telling him their names.

"My name's Hannah," said the green-haired girl, "and what you said is just so right on."

Alessa and Hannah got into a discussion about the class president election campaign. They talked about slogans and posters, which Eddie understood, and about podcasts and text blasts, which he didn't. He began to like the idea the more he thought about it. He'd always been president or vice president of his class back home. Just being a candidate was a good way to meet people and make new friends. Since Tom hadn't been in this school very long, most people probably wouldn't notice how different he was.

He missed Tom. He thought, *I wish we could have spent more time together.* Tom seemed like a fearless guy, gutsy, and so smart. A cool brother.

He heard a sweet, silvery voice say, "I think it's wonderful that you're running." He recognized it instantly: Merlyn, the new cheerleader.

But that was back there, not here.

He turned. It *was* Merlyn, all right, with her long black hair that covered one of her bright green eyes. What was she doing here?

Merlyn said, "This school needs fresh blood."

"If you're a vampire," said Alessa. She was scowling.

Merlyn ignored her. "And here's my campaign

contribution." She put six dollar bills on the table in front of Eddie. "We need to perform together again. Closer to the election."

She laughed and walked away.

"What was that all about?" said Alessa.

"Beats me," said Eddie. *Have to ask Tom about this.* And how could she be in two places? *Merlyn must be a monitor.*

"You're hot," said the boy with the raccoon eyes. "It's that YouTube clip."

"Give her a break," said Hannah. "Maybe she's a Greenie, too."

"That Gossip Girl is just playing him," said Alessa. She was glaring at Eddie. "When did you perform together? What was that money for?"

Eddie looked right into Alessa's eyes. "I don't know what she was talking about."

Alessa muttered something under her breath, but she nodded and looked down.

People usually believed Eddie. He was glad they believed him on this planet, too.

Suddenly, he felt sick. Was it Merlyn, the turkey wrap, or was Tom landing? Eddie hoped his brother was all right.

THIRTY-THREE

I N the afternoon there was a class called tech lab. Everyone sat in front of a computer. Alessa showed Eddie how to turn it on. That was as far as he got. Kids were "Googling." He almost laughed out loud at that word. Sounded dirty. Turned out it was a way of looking up things fast. He wondered if you could get sports scores.

In science, the teacher was talking about "climate change." The planet was getting hotter, and she said most scientists thought it was people's fault. How could people change the weather? Eddie wondered.

In history, the teacher used her computer to put a chart on the wall. She called it Mrs. Rupp's Timeline. She was asking when the wars in Afghanistan and Iraq started. Eddie didn't know where those countries were, much less that there were wars there.

Then he followed Alessa to the auditorium for the election committee meeting. He sat there shivering, even though it was warm.

"What's wrong?" said Alessa. "Are you sick?"

He couldn't tell her he was sharing the slipping flu with the real Tom. "The pills," he said.

She put her head close to his and whispered, "I went to a shrink once and I took pills like that."

"What happened?"

"They didn't help me the way they're helping you. You're so much more chill. I can't believe you're running for office after such a short time in school."

You don't even know how *short*, he thought. *And this isn't the real Tom's kind of thing.* In just the little time he had spent with him, Eddie could tell that Tom was a loner kind of guy who kept to himself, reading, doing his tech stuff, and playing the violin. Tom didn't have friends. Eddie wondered how many people would vote for him. He'd have to act different from Tom to get votes. But then he wouldn't be Tom, he'd be Eddie. His head felt as mixed up as his stomach. He wished he was as smart as his brother.

A funny-looking guy came strutting out on stage. He was dressed like a kid even though he was old. He wore tight dungarees, sneakers, and a T-shirt. He stopped suddenly, pretending he had just noticed all the kids sitting in the auditorium. "Fancy meeting you here."

He looked so familiar.

I know that guy.

"Dr. Traum is a buffoon," said Alessa.

"Dr. Traum?"

"Earth to Tom. Dr. Traum. The school psychologist? Our orchestra teacher?"

How about my *school psychologist and the football coach?* "Sorry, Alessa, I forgot."

"'Sokay. It's your pills. Uh-oh. Not her, too." The history teacher walked out on stage. "Mrs. Rupp is an alien species."

Eddie went on alert until he figured out that Alessa was making a joke.

"Let's settle down, people," said Mrs. Rupp. "Dr. Traum and I will be the election commissioners, and I can assure you that this will be a fair process. Nominations are in order for seventh grade student council."

Since Eddie didn't know any of the kids, the nominations didn't mean much to him. He tuned out, wondering about Tom. Finally, Mrs. Rupp and Dr. Traum got to seventh grade class president.

Alessa jumped up. "He hasn't been here very long, but you've seen him on YouTube and you know he fights for his rights. He'll fight for yours, too. Let's give it up for Tom Canty!"

Merlyn seconded the nomination. There was some applause and some whistles. *Like when the team needs a touchdown and you get a first down,* thought Eddie.

Alessa pulled him to his feet and raised one of his arms. A little more applause.

That felt good. Not like throwing a touchdown, but good.

He noticed that both Mrs. Rupp and Dr. Traum were shaking their heads.

THIRTY-FOUR

ALESSA made Eddie sit through orchestra practice even though he couldn't play. Dr. Traum smiled at him but left him alone. No question, it was the same guy. *Got to talk to Tom about this. And to Grandpa.* Dr. Traum and Merlyn on both planets! Thinking about that made his head ache.

Alessa's mom dropped him off at Tom's house. There was a car in the driveway, one of those truck cars, and the lights were on in the kitchen, but no one was around. He ate some leftover Chinese food, cold and greasy—the way he liked it—made himself a peanut butter and mustard sandwich, poured a glass of milk, and went upstairs. While he ate and drank, he tried to turn on Tom's TV. Couldn't figure it out. He felt lousy. He lay down on top of the bed.

Catch a few zzz's.

When he woke up, it was dark and the TV was blasting in the living room. He went downstairs. Keith — it had to be him, the Lump, a big guy with red whiskers — was stretched out on the sofa with a can of beer balanced on his stomach, watching a baseball game on the biggest TV Eddie had ever seen. And it was in color! Amazing picture. He couldn't stop staring at it. The players looked huge. They weren't wearing baseball stockings. Their pants went down to their shoes, which weren't all black.

You could see their faces clearly. You could see the sweat on the pitcher's face. The batter needed a shave. He swung, a grounder to deep short, a bang-bang play at first. And then it played again. Instantly. Twice.

"When did they start doing that?" said Eddie.

"Baseball? Around two hundred years ago."

Eddie laughed. That was pretty funny. "No, playing it over again right away."

"Instant replay?" The Lump took a sip of his beer and looked at Eddie as if he wasn't sure whether he was being a wise guy or not. "In the sixties."

Too bad, thought Eddie. *I'll have to wait a few years.*

"You interested all of a sudden? Or just for the postseason?"

I've been a big fan all my life, Eddie wanted to say, but he caught himself in time. *The real Tom isn't a fan.*

"Who's playing?"

"L.A. and the Mets."

"L.A.?"

"The Dodgers."

"They're in Brooklyn."

"Not since 1957."

"They moved?"

"Obviously. You really do hate sports."

I love sports, Eddie thought. *In the last century.* "And the Mets?"

"They started in 1962. Before your time."

After my time, Eddie thought. *Have to wait five more years. Better keep my mouth shut.*

"Grab a soda, watch with me," said Keith. "You might like it."

The only Cokes in the fridge were Diet Cokes, but he took one. He broke off a little ring on top trying to open it, and when he had to use an opener, he nearly crushed the can in his hand, it was so soft. And it tasted funny. He didn't like it, but he sipped at it while he watched the game.

"Who are you rooting for?" he asked Keith.

"Doesn't matter. Yankees are my team."

"Me, too."

Keith squinted at him. "Who's your favorite Yankee?"

It sounded like a trick question.

"The Mick."

"Mantle? He died before you were born."

Mickey Mantle dead? Eddie felt sad. He loved Mickey Mantle. He practiced switch hitting to be like him. "I saw pictures of him," he said. "Great swing. So fast."

"Watch this guy," said Keith, pointing at the screen. "The real deal. He's got power, and he doesn't strike out much."

They watched the batter punch a double to the opposite field.

"Really sits on the pitch," said Eddie. "You gotta have great eyes to wait until the last second like that. Probably can't fool him with a curve."

Keith stared at Eddie.

Uh-oh, thought Eddie, *I'd better get out of here before I say something that makes him suspicious.* "I really need to finish my homework. See you in the morning, Keith."

"Sure."

Eddie could tell he liked being called Keith by someone he thought was Tom, maybe for the first time. He gave Eddie a smile and a thumbs-up.

"Is there a game tomorrow?"

"Yep."

"Maybe I could watch with you."

"I'd like that," Keith said.

Upstairs, Eddie thought about trying again to figure out Tom's TV set and watch the game, but he decided he couldn't make any more mistakes. Maybe he could get Alessa to show him how to use the TV, the computer, and the phone, if Tom's little phone was still around. Too much to learn too fast.

The pills would be a good excuse for a while, he thought, but eventually he'd need a better reason not to be using all these gadgets.

THIRTY-FIVE

I n the car to school, Alessa was thumbing her telephone.

"What are you doing?"

"I'm surfing for ideas."

"Don't get wet."

Eddie thought it was a pretty good joke, but Alessa just squinted at him. "Surfing means looking for something on the Internet, you idiot. Did you forget that, too?"

"What are you looking for?"

"Middle school election campaigns."

Eddie looked over her shoulder. The little screen read, "Rule Number One: School elections are not fair."

"Everything should be fair."

"You want to win, right?"

"Not if it's unfair," said Eddie.

"Life's unfair," said Alessa.

"Sports are fair."

"Right. Like steroids."

"What's that?"

Alessa sighed. "Google it." She sounded impatient.

He was annoyed. She knew he didn't know how to Google. "Maybe things would be better if people stopped Googling all the time."

"C'mon, you sound like somebody from another century," said Alessa. Her thumbs were dancing on her phone. "Besides, what would we do without the Internet?"

"Talk to each other? Try to get along better?"

Alessa didn't look up. "That'll be the day."

The teachers were having a conference in the auditorium, so the seventh grade was marched into the gym to play dodgeball. Eddie liked dodgeball, but he could see why kids hated it when Britzky yelled "Britzkyball!" and started nailing them. The teachers in the gym were busy thumbing their tiny telephones and couldn't care less.

Britzky kept glancing at Eddie but didn't throw the ball his way. Instead, he kept trying to nail Alessa and the kids who sat at her cafeteria table. Alessa didn't move very fast, and she got whacked in the face and went into a corner so people wouldn't see her cry. Eddie felt sorry for her. Tom would have done something. Probably with one of his electronic devices.

What should I do? Eddie thought. *It's not like I'm on Britzky's side or anything, but Alessa did make that nasty crack about his face, and even though she's a girl, she should know you can't go around insulting people and not think they're going to get mad and try to get even.*

But she was Tom's friend and she was helping him. She was on Eddie's team.

He thought about decking Britzky, but Tom was on probation, so he'd probably get suspended. He could tell Britzky to stop, but if he didn't, what would Eddie do next? Tom wouldn't run to a teacher.

What would Captain Eddie do? If a guy on the team messed up or had a bad attitude, it never did much good to punch him out or even yell at him. You take him aside and talk to him privately, or at least show him the right way by your own actions.

Sorry, Tom. Maybe we have to do this the Captain Eddie way.

When Britzky pegged the ball at Hannah, the green-haired girl, Eddie ran out on the court, leaped up, and grabbed it in midair. It was like intercepting a pass. It caught everybody's attention. The gym got quiet. Britzky faced Eddie, all tensed up. Eddie thought Britzky looked like he wasn't sure if he should start searching for a place to hide or get ready to fight.

Relax, Eddie thought, *I'm not going to act like you.*

He shouted, "You win, Britzky. Game's over."

He dribbled the dodgeball between his legs, did his double spin, and fired a jumper at the nearest basket, which was almost a half-court away. It wasn't a pretty shot; it was no nothing-but-net, just a soft bank off the backboard. But it did the job. The dodgeball spun in the rim and fell through.

Crowd goes wild!

One of the gym teachers came over. "I thought you played the violin."

"Not right now," Eddie said.

For the rest of the gym period, while everybody stood and watched, the gym teacher made Eddie shoot baskets from different places on the floor with a real basketball. Eddie thought about all the hours with Dad at the hoop on the garage. When Dad was around, they'd get out there even if they had to shovel snow off the driveway. Eddie pretended Dad was in the crowd in the gym cheering him on, and he sank almost everything

—layups, jumpers, set shots, even his alley-oop. He ignored the slipping flu symptoms.

"Can you drain some free throws for me?" said the gym teacher.

"Better believe it."

Dad always made Eddie finish a practice by shooting a hundred free throws. He was sinking sixty percent when Dad disappeared, and now he was up to almost eighty percent. Dad said the foul shot was the one thing you could totally control on the court and there was no excuse for not being solid at the line. It showed discipline.

This was for Dad.

Eddie set up, talking to himself: *Fingertips on the ball, keep your back and arms straight to get as much reach as possible, lower the ball between your legs . . .*

"You kidding me?" said the gym teacher. "You think you're Rick Barry?"

"Who?"

"Before your time. We don't shoot underhand free throws anymore." He held his hands up and pretended to toss a ball. "Overhand."

Eddie thought, *The real Eddie would do what the coach says, but I'm not Eddie now. I'm Tom. And besides, this was how Dad taught me.*

He threw up the ball underhand.

Swish.

The gym teacher just stared. Eddie didn't move. The ball bounced itself into a corner. Everybody was waiting to see what happened next.

Finally, the gym teacher shrugged, picked up the basketball, and bounced it to Eddie, who gave him a little salute, spun the ball on his fingertips, set, and shot. *Swish.*

He sank seventeen in a row underhand before the PA system announced that the teacher meeting had ended and that students should return to their classrooms. Eddie noticed Britzky glaring at him over his shoulder as he hurried out. This wasn't over yet.

The gym teacher walked up grinning and raised his hand. When Eddie just stared at it, he said, "High-five, my man." Eddie figured it out and slapped the gym teacher's palm. "We'll be starting tryouts for the team in a couple of weeks. What position do you play?"

"Point guard."

"Outstanding. Be there or be square." He winked. "And try to stay out of trouble, Canty. We could really use you."

Alessa caught up to Eddie in the hall afterward. "That was awesome. This election will be a slam dunk."

"A what?"

"I'm texting the Tom Canty for President Committee

right now." She was thumbing away. "We've got to come up with a slogan."

"You're going to do that on the phone?"

"You want to waste your time in meetings?"

"That's how people get things done—they talk to each other face-to-face . . ."

"They babble away, have ego trips, waste time. You want to have to sit and look at some dork?"

"Maybe if people did that, the world wouldn't be so screwed up."

"That is so two-point-oh."

"What does that mean?"

"Here's one." She read from the little screen. "'Let Tom quarterback the seventh grade.' Not bad."

"This school doesn't have a football team."

"Oh. Right." She hit a button.

"We need people to work together to solve the problems," he said.

"What kind of problems? This is middle school, not the Middle East."

"I think all these gadgets get in the way."

"Are you kidding? People never talked before. Now we have Facebook, Twitter, new ways to stay in touch."

"I think everybody's talking to themselves." Eddie started to get excited. "They should turn off all the machines so they can hear each other."

"Never happen." She looked at Eddie. "But it might make a campaign slogan."

While he was trying to think of what to say next, he realized that the flu was gone. He felt good.

Tom must have landed.

THIRTY-SIX

A FLASHLIGHT dazzled my eyes. The flu was gone. I was hungry. I hadn't eaten Grandpa's turkey wrap. I was sitting against a tree, hugging my violin bag.

A familiar voice said, "Everything okay, sonny?" A strong hand pulled me to my feet. "Chop-chop."

"Grandpa!"

He held me by my shoulders and looked me over. "None the worse."

"What's going on?"

He hurried me toward a parked car. "You were at Boy Scout camp and you wandered off a trail and fell down a cliff. You were missing for hours."

"I don't remember any of that."

"It never happened. It's the cover story for why you have amnesia."

"Amnesia?"

"Just relax. You're Eddie now." Grandpa opened the trunk of the car and pulled a Boy Scout uniform out of a duffel bag. "Put this on. Hurry."

He had to help me with the yellow neckerchief. Then he rubbed some dirt on the uniform and tore one of the sleeves.

"Why did you do that?"

"You fell down a cliff, remember?"

"No."

"You're not supposed to remember. Amnesia. Don't forget."

Grandpa opened the passenger door of his car, a red and white Chevy, the kind you see in old movies. I said, "Cool vintage ride."

"Two years old," said Grandpa proudly. "A Bel Air."

I remembered it was 1957 here.

Grandpa drove down a street of identical houses. In the streetlights they looked like square white ghost boxes. How could you know which one was yours?

We pulled up in front of one of them.

"This is it, Eddie."

"I'm Tom. What the hell is going on?"

"Watch your mouth." He was pulling me out of the car and across a little front lawn to the house. "We don't like that kind of language here."

A dog raced toward us, barking.

"That's your dog, Buddy."

I never had a dog.

The dog stopped, growled at me. I guess I didn't smell like Eddie. Or he could tell I don't like dogs, especially floppy-eared cocker spaniels like him who think they're so cute.

"Work on him," said Grandpa. "Give him treats."

We went inside the house, through a living room where the furniture was covered with see-through plastic. There was a painting over the fireplace: Eddie wearing a Cub Scout uniform, with Dad on one side and Grandpa on the other.

"Would you like a sandwich?"

My stomach reminded me how hungry I was. "Sure. Unless you have pizza."

Grandpa looked at his watch. "Kinda late. Sal's is closed."

"Domino online is pretty quick." I stopped when I saw him staring at me. "Frozen is okay." Another stare.

"This is 1957."

"Sorry. Since I hit my head . . ."

"That's good," said Grandpa. "You always were a quick study."

"How about peanut butter and mustard?" I said.

"You, too?" Grandpa rolled his eyes but made me the sandwich, on white bread. The dog kept growling until

I gave him a little piece. He managed to nip my finger.

"Buddy was really worried about you, Eddie. He just sat at the door and cried the whole time you were gone."

"He knows, doesn't he?"

"But he can't talk. You'd better get to bed. Slipping takes a lot out of you."

I followed him upstairs. Eddie's room was smaller than mine, and neater. There were maps on the wall and posters of Mickey Mantle and two other guys—Paul Hornung and Bob Cousy. Mantle was the only one I'd heard of. The biggest map was of the United States. I noticed that Hawaii and Alaska weren't on it.

I went into the bathroom down the hall. It was so pink, I could only pee. And I was thinking about all the questions I had for Grandpa.

When I came out, Grandpa was waiting in the hall. "I know you've got a ton of questions, but get a good night's sleep first. You'll need it."

"Just one question?"

When he nodded, I said, "What was Dad like?"

"He was terrific. Smart like you and nice like your brother. And when you grow up, both of you are going to be like him. Now to bed."

I got into bed with my clothes on. I was exhausted. I tried to think about Hawaii and Alaska, but I fell right asleep.

THIRTY-SEVEN

NEARMONT, N.J.
1957

I WAS swarmed when I got on the school bus. Kids cheered and patted me, and gave me little shoulder punches. Girls hugged me. Even the bus driver gave me a thumbs-up. It made me uncomfortable. I wasn't used to that kind of attention, and I'd never been touched so much by kids in school. I'm not a touchy-feely kind of guy.

I was glad that Eddie was so popular, but I was a little jealous. All this friendship was about him, not me. I wondered how he was doing. I hoped Alessa was helping him. Where was this guy Ronnie?

The kids cleared space so I could sit down near the front. I was holding my violin backpack, but no one asked me what was in it. They probably thought it was filled with sports equipment. They crowded around. Everybody wanted to ask about what happened. I tried to act like Eddie would, humble and patient. "I wish I could remember. Honest. The doctor said I have amnesia."

"Amnesia? I forgot what that means," shouted a skinny kid who wormed his way through the crowd in the aisle. He nodded and grinned at the laugh he got. He looked like he could be the class clown. He had wild, messy hair and a small sharp face, a little dirty but almost too pretty for a boy. He was wearing a ratty old yellow sweater-shirt and skinny black pants. Scuffed boots. This had to be Ronnie.

"Ronnie?"

"You were expecting Elvis?" He started singing something about forgetting to remember.

This is the guy I'm supposed to depend on—Eddie's sidekick?

He looked ten years old. But I put on my sincere face. "Ronnie, I'm really going to need your help today," I said. "You've got to remind me of everything. Show me where to go."

"You got it." He looked eager and excited. "I'm your sidekick."

"Right. Like Han Solo and Chewbacca," I said.

"Who?"

Whoops, no *Star Wars* yet. "Like the Lone Ranger and Tonto."

"Better believe it, kemo sabe," he said.

THIRTY-EIGHT

T HE bus pulled up at school. It looked like a couple of the middle schools I'd been to, only newer. It had the same fountain out front I remembered from the Nearmont Middle School on EarthOne.

Teachers patted me in the hall, told me they had been worried sick.

Ronnie was my shadow. He gave me nudges and signals where to go. At homeroom, kids clapped and the teacher gave me a kiss on the cheek. Back home, a teacher might get arrested for that. Not that I would know; no teacher had ever kissed *me* before. Still hadn't. She thought she was kissing Eddie. That helped me get used to it. It was Eddie that everyone thought they were touching. It wasn't so bad.

Bells rang and everyone stood up for the Pledge of Allegiance. The flag looked different to me. It took me a while to figure it out. It only had forty-eight stars. That's why Hawaii and Alaska weren't on that map. They weren't states yet! When were they made states? *I need some dates, Mrs. Rupp.*

On the wall where most classrooms had a picture of the president was a photo of a smiling old white man.

I nudged Ronnie. "Who's that?"

"I like Ike," he said.

"Ike?"

"The president," said Ronnie. "Dwight D. Eisenhower."

I clicked through the list of presidents in my head. Dad and I used to quiz each other on presidents, state capitals, and planets the way other kids and dads did batting averages and Super Bowl winners. Probably like Eddie and Dad.

"Eisenhower was president fifty years ago."

When Ronnie looked at me like I was crazy, I remembered that Hawaii and Alaska were the last two territories to be made states.

I scanned the room until I found the calendar. It was open to October 1957. *Wish I could Google 1957, find out what's happening.* I thought about Mrs. Rupp's timeline. Didn't we talk about some big technology thing in 1957? Space . . . Russians . . . My mind was still a little shook up from the slip trip.

Everything seemed slower here. Teachers dawdled, as if they were in no hurry to get us ready to take tests. They wore suits and ties or dresses. Maybe this was Dress-up Day. No jeans anywhere. Kids took their time in the halls. Even the big round clocks on the walls seemed to be ticking off lazy seconds. Through my first two classes, math and Spanish, my legs jiggled under my desk, which happens when I'm nervous or bored. I was both. How can you be both? Math was easy, and Spanish sounded like a baby talking French, the language I was taking back home.

I was uncomfortable in the clothes that Grandpa had laid out for me. Sand-colored desert boots, brown corduroy pants, and a yellow and black shirt. Everything itched, especially the pants. I hadn't worn corduroy since I was a little kid. It gets damp between your thighs and makes your underwear crawl up into your crack. In science, I was squirming around in my seat trying to rub the underwear out.

"Edward, did you want to answer this question?"

I hadn't been paying attention, and I didn't react to the name until Ronnie kicked me. I looked up. The teacher was standing in front of a big roll-down chart of the solar system. No PowerPoint here.

I said, "I'm sorry. I forgot the question."

"What are the planets of our solar system?"

That was easy. "Mercury, Venus, Earth, Mars, Jupiter, Saturn, Uranus, and Neptune."

"You forgot one, Edward."

"That's it," I said.

The teacher shook her head. "Merlyn?"

It was her! The same long black hair covering her face. What was she doing here? She said, "Pluto."

"Very good," said the teacher.

"Pluto's not a planet," I said. "It's a star."

"Where did you hear that?" said the teacher.

A little warning bell rang in my head, but I couldn't stop myself. "Pluto's too small to be a planet. It's a dwarf planet, all ice and rock."

"Pluto is a planet on this planet," said Merlyn, smiling at me. "Maybe not on whatever planet you come from."

The class grumbled at her. I guess it didn't like anyone making fun of its hero, Eddie.

"Amnesia," said Ronnie. "Anything can happen after a knock on the head. And Eddie's had two, one in football and one at Scout camp."

"That's true," said the teacher. She frowned. "How do you feel, Edward?"

"I'm fine," I said.

The teacher came over and put her hand on my forehead. She smelled of talcum powder. "No fever."

The bell rang.

"Have you been to your doctor?" asked the teacher.

I nodded.

"No need," said Merlyn. "I have a new trick to examine his brain at the lunchtime talent show."

Outside in the hallway, I said to Ronnie, "What's with that Merlyn?"

"Search me. She's new."

THIRTY-NINE

THE cafeteria was a crummy hole. The floor was yellow linoleum with black scabs. Kids sat on gray metal benches at long gray metal picnic tables, like in the old black-and-white prison movies I watched on Turner Classic. I wasn't hungry anyway.

Grandpa had made me a great breakfast. Scrambled eggs, bacon, hot buttered toast, cold orange juice, and milk. It was delicious. I wasn't used to eating so much for breakfast.

"You sit over there," said Ronnie, pointing to a table in the center of the cafeteria.

You could tell it was a hotshot table: student government types in chinos and blue button-down shirts, jocks in team jerseys, and girls wearing skirts and two matching sweaters. Around us were thug tables and freak tables and rebel tables. Not much had changed over the years. Except the shoes. Kids were wearing dorky-looking shoes, a lot of brown leather and desert boots. I guess Nike and Skechers hadn't been invented yet.

Ronnie started to slink away.

"Where you going?"

He pointed his chin toward a table in the corner packed with fat kids, goofy-looking kids, boys with pens, pencils, and little rulers in plastic holders in their shirt pockets.

I grabbed his skinny arm and pulled him toward the hot table. "You're staying with me."

"They won't let me," he said.

"Let 'em stop us."

No one said anything as I climbed over the bench and made room for Ronnie and my violin bag. He didn't look happy, but I needed him close. I could tell that the kids at the table weren't happy, either, but Eddie got his way in this school. *I wish I had spent more time with him.* On EarthOne we would have called him a people person.

Grandpa had packed me a huge roast beef sandwich on a roll, an apple, and cookies. Ronnie had a slice of bologna and a slice of cheese on white bread. He stuffed his sandwich in his pocket and started to get up. "I gotta go, Eddie."

I pulled him down and gave him half my roast beef

sandwich. The way he ate it, I wondered if he had had any breakfast.

One of the jocks pointed at my violin bag. "What's in there?"

"My violin," I said.

Kids at the table started laughing like I had cracked a great joke.

"Gonna play for us?" a girl said.

"If you're lucky."

"In the talent show?" She pointed at Merlyn, who was fussing with her little folding table and collapsible top hat. "Miss Conceited thinks she's going to win."

Merlyn was definitely the girl from the park. How had she gotten here? The same way I got here?

Then I remembered Grandpa had said that Dr. Traum was probably a monitor because he could be two places at the same time. So Merlyn was probably a monitor. *I'd better be careful with her.*

The PA system started crackling, and some kid announced the seventh grade lunchtime open talent show. Teachers went around shushing people.

At one side of the cafeteria, a little band set up and three girls climbed up on a table with a microphone and sang a sappy song about "Tammy." They were terrible, but they must have been popular because they got a lot of applause. Then a kid tap-danced. Then a girl in a ballet outfit danced. A guy sang "All Shook Up," and kids screamed when he did a little wiggle with it. Ronnie was singing along with him.

Suddenly, there was a drum roll from the band and Merlyn climbed up on the table. She was wearing the black top hat. She set up her little table on top of the big table.

Merlyn was as good as I remembered her. Just like a real magician on TV, she kept talking so you couldn't concentrate on what she was doing — juggling four red balls, pulling a rabbit doll out of her hat, doing card tricks. Kids came up and she plucked coins out of their ears. Then she said, "I know some of you think I made Eddie Tudor disappear. We're all so glad he's back, even if he's lost his memory. So come on up, Eddie. Do a trick with me."

I stood up.

Ronnie grabbed my arm. "Cool your jets. Don't do it."

Everybody was looking at me. I couldn't wimp out. I picked up my pack and walked across the cafeteria, slow, like a gunfighter, and climbed up on the table next to Merlyn.

"I see you brought your violin," she said. Everybody laughed.

She pulled the red scarf out of her hat and started

pretending to push it into one of my ears. Only this time it really felt like something was going into my head. How did she do that? Could aliens do things like that? It was creepy, but I didn't pull away. Then she reached around my head and pulled the red scarf out of my other ear. What a strange feeling.

"Just as I thought," said Merlyn. "Eddie's head is still empty."

Teachers were laughing. Everybody was laughing except Ronnie. His head was lowered.

Poor guy, I thought, *he really loves Eddie.*

I waited until the laughter died down. "Thank you for cleaning my head, Merlyn, so I can play better." I opened my pack and took out my violin. People gasped.

I took my time tuning up, thinking of what to play. Then I remembered the song Alessa's mom had been playing in the car. "Let me dedicate this song to Merlyn the Magician."

I faced her as I played and sang:

Tough girlz, think you're cruel.
Tough girlz, too cool for school.
Tough girlz, you just foolz.
Tough girlz, tough girlz.

The cafeteria went crazy. I got a standing O. Clapping and stomping and cheering. For me. For *Tom*. It felt great. I hoped Eddie was feeling some of the chilly happy fingers playing up and down my spine.

One of the teachers held a vote. By applause, I won the open talent show by a landslide. I thought about Mrs. Rupp's Timeline. How many years to go until the song "Tough Girlz" gets written? I looked at Merlyn. She winked.

What's her game?

FORTY

NEARMONT, N.J.
1957

You didn't tell me Alessa was a Negro.

Is that a problem for you, Eddie?

No, but I never knew one before.

Just like us only darker. Didn't Dad or Grandpa talk about that?

Grandpa talked about Jackie all the time. He loved Jackie.

Who's Jackie?

You kidding? Jackie Robinson.

The baseball player?

The first Negro player in the major leagues, April 15, 1947.

Timeline Rupp's gonna love you.

I liked that timeline, Tom, especially the stuff that happened after my time.

We could bet on the World Series.

What do you mean?

You could Google who wins the Series in 1957, and I could bet on it.

That would be wrong.

Don't be such a Boy Scout, Eddie. By the way, we don't say Negro anymore, we say African American.

This kid Britzky . . .

The kid I bombed. He picks on Alessa.

That's going to be okay.

How come?

I can make him a friend.

Some friend. What's the deal with Ronnie?

He's my little pal. Yours now.

You pick him out of a Dumpster?

A what?

The garbage.

That's not nice.

The way he dresses. He smells bad. And he looks like a girl.

He's a stand-up guy. You can count on him.

I gave him half my lunch.

I always do that. I don't think he lives anywhere.

He's homeless?

He won't talk about it. Hey, how's Buddy? I really miss him.

He knows. He growls at me.

Give him treats.

He tries to bite me.

We'd better stop. Grandpa said not to talk more than five minutes at a time, the monitors could be trying to tune in.

Eddie . . . ?

FORTY-ONE

THE stars blinked off. They looked just like the ones in the backyard on my planet. I went back into the house. Grandpa was watching TV on a black-and-white set. He kept jiggling the two tall silver antennas on top of the set and still got lousy reception. No dish or cable here yet. Or color. He had to keep getting up to adjust the sound. No remote.

"It's on," he said.

An announcer in a suit and tie appeared on the screen and said, "Here he is: the one, the only . . . ," and the studio audience screamed, "Groucho!" A funny-looking guy with a mustache who walked like a duck came out. And then a wooden duck came down from the ceiling with a hundred-dollar bill in its mouth and the announcer said that tonight's secret word was *space*.

The show was called *You Bet Your Life,* and it wasn't

too lame. Groucho made jokes with his guests, who had to answer questions to win up to $10,000. Chump change. Grandpa loved the show. He laughed every time Groucho wiggled his eyebrows or waggled his cigar. By the time the show was over, Grandpa had tears in his eyes from laughing so much.

I guess I must have been looking at him weirdly because he said, "Not a ton of real smart stuff back here in 1957."

"At least you got all your marbles in 1957, Grandpa."

He laughed. "That's the kind of crack your dad would make."

I took a breath. "Grandpa, do you think he could be alive?"

"Why do you ask that?"

When adults answer your question with a question, they're stalling for time. I felt an excitement deep in my stomach come up into my chest. "He's alive, isn't he? He's hiding from the monitors."

"You're a smart boy." He gave me a hug. "Now go to bed."

I could tell he wasn't going to say anything else, so I went upstairs. I wondered if I'd be able to go to sleep.

I felt funny using Eddie's toothbrush. Instead, I just put toothpaste on my finger and rubbed it over my teeth. I got into bed in my underwear.

Dad *had* to be alive. The monitors were hunting the rebel leader. What could I do in the fight against the monitors?

I remembered that in one of the Mark Twain books Grandpa and I read, *A Connecticut Yankee in King Arthur's Court*, the hero beat the evil magician Merlin because he knew there was going to be an eclipse of the sun on a certain date.

Had anything like that happened in 1957? Would I remember if it had? I was dead without Google. If only I could get online here.

I dug my phone out of the violin bag. No signal. And it was running out of juice. I had a charger, but so what? I plugged it in anyway and charged the phone. Old habit.

Eddie had a marked-up calendar on the wall. Today was Thursday, October 3, 1957. I needed Google, Mrs. Rupp's Timeline, something.

You Bet Your Life.

The magic word was *space*.

Something really important was hiding in a fold of my brain. Just when I thought I was getting close, I fell asleep.

FORTY-TWO

EDDIE persuaded Alessa to take the school bus with him by telling her it would be good for the campaign. They'd meet more kids every day, get to know them. Her mom wasn't sure it was a good idea, but she trusted him to protect Alessa. Eddie didn't like riding in their big truck of a car. He was used to riding in buses with a bunch of kids, fooling around, making friends.

Alessa was staring at her little screen. Her lips were trembling.

"What's up, pup?"

She handed him her telephone. The words on the screen were:

KISS YR PIZZA BUTT BYBY.

BRAINDEAD CAN'T SAVE YOU.

"Who's it from?"

"Britzky," she said. "He's a cyberbully."

"Cyberbully?'

"Maybe you *are* brain dead." She was very upset. "Sorry. It's not you. It's your pills."

The bus pulled up at the school.

Eddie looked at the big stone fountain on the sidewalk outside the school. At his junior high school, the after-school fights were held by the fountain. They were called showdowns. Eddie didn't fight much. A jock rarely had to. But if you did fight, the whole team showed up to cover your back.

"You should report it," said Eddie.

"I can't prove it's him."

He gave her back the phone and jumped off the bus. "I'll think of something," he said. He was feeling more confident since sinking those baskets. He felt more like himself instead of a fake Tom. He bounced his rubber ball a few times.

He followed Alessa to a wall of lockers. Before he even asked, she told him his combination. There was a pink slip of paper inside his locker. It read: *You're so gay.* Eddie laughed. It was true, he was feeling pretty good. He wondered if it was from Merlyn. He always got notes like that from girls in his old school.

"You think that's funny?" said Alessa, who had read the note over his shoulder.

She was starting to get on his nerves. "Don't be jealous."

"Do you even know what that means?"

"It means I'm, you know, in a good mood, happy."

She just stared at him. "It's from Britzky. He'd text you if you had a phone. It's a bias crime to write that. It's not allowed."

"To call someone happy?"

"Is it really the pills, or are you trying to punk everybody out?"

"What?"

She gave off a big sigh. It was like the air rushing out of a blow-up mattress at Scout camp. "'Gay' means homosexual."

Eddie wasn't really sure what "homosexual" meant. He did know it wasn't considered nice to use the word back home. "So what's the big deal? 'Sticks and stones can break my bones but names will never hurt me.' Ever hear that?"

"Sure they can hurt you. People use words and names to scare you, to bully you, to turn people against you."

"So maybe I should report it."

"You can't. It would be wimpy. You would lose your YouTube cred."

It took him a moment to figure that out. She was talking about Tom's reputation for being tough. *But I've got a reputation, too. I'm Captain Eddie, a leader. I don't run for help. People run to me for help.*

Cyberbullies. Hurting people you hardly know over the airwaves. *It'll come to my planet in fifty years.*

An idea began to form.

He followed Alessa to history. Mrs. Rupp made her computer do its thing, and a chart of dates went up on the wall. One of them was October 4, 1957. That was tomorrow. The chart was moving, and all he could see was something about a spaceship. Mrs. Rupp said the wrong people conquered space. The aliens? Mrs. Rupp glared at Eddie a few times, but she never called on him.

Tom needed to know about the spaceship tomorrow, Eddie thought. But meanwhile, his idea grew into a plan, filled his head. It was hard to keep two things spinning in his brain at the same time.

FORTY-THREE

I've got to tell you something, Tom.

What?

Something big's going to happen tomorrow.

You're telling me!

Right. A showdown with Britzky. And I've got this plan

to . . .

No. Here, Eddie. On EarthTwo.

Oh, yeah, I almost forgot, Tom. A spaceship. Mrs. Rupp said

the wrong people conquered space.

That's it! Sputnik.

Tom? Tom?

FORTY-FOUR

GRANDPA was pedaling hard on a stationary bike when Eddie arrived. He was the only person in the assisted living facility's little gym. His T-shirt was drenched with sweat. Eddie could hear music howling out of the little white things in his ears. Ear buds, Alessa had called them.

He started right off telling Grandpa about his plan.

"What?" Grandpa pulled out the buds. "I'm listening to 'Welcome to the Jungle.' Guns N' Roses. Really gets your blood boiling."

He swung off the bike and walked to a rack of weights. "I believe in lighter poundage, more reps. How about you?"

"More weight for football, less for basketball and baseball."

Grandpa started pumping his biceps. "So, how's it going?"

"Pretty good. I'm going to run for class president. And I've got this idea . . ."

"Excellent. Give you a chance to eyeball for more monitors."

"What do they look like?"

Grandpa stopped pumping and lowered his voice. "Like humans. They have bright green eyes that allow them to transmit video back to Homeplace."

"Homeplace?"

"That's what we call our planet."

"Is that where you and Dad are from?"

He nodded.

"What's it like?"

Two old ladies came into the gym and stood near Grandpa. They bent over and touched their toes and peeked at him. He started pumping again and grinned at them.

Grandpa winked at Eddie and said loudly, "Thanks for coming, sonny, whoever you are." He started talking to the old ladies. It was as if Eddie had disappeared.

Eddie got lost on the ride home. His mind felt as fuddled as it had during the slip. He'd wanted to run his idea past Grandpa. Now he really had to talk to Tom.

He tried for an hour in the backyard. He might have stayed out all night if Keith hadn't heard him shouting in the garden and told him to come in and watch the game.

FORTY-FIVE

O N the school bus, Eddie said to Alessa, "Do me a favor? Send Britzky a whaddyacallit. Tell him to meet me at the fountain at three."

"What for?"

"A showdown. It's like *High Noon, Shane, 3:10 to Yuma.* You see that?"

"With Russell Crowe?"

"No, it was Glenn Ford," Eddie said. "Can you send it?"

"Get serious, Tom. You're on probation. And you're running for office. Fighting's not allowed."

"Who says I'm going to fight him?"

"Oh, right. You're calling him out for a *poetry slam.*" She sounded sarcastic. "Like you can make a rhyme at any time."

Eddie laughed. "I'm a poet and you don't know it.

Please. Trust me. Just send it. And send it to a few other people."

"Why?"

"So he can't back out."

By the time he got off the bus, he could feel the pressure building, like before a big game.

In the halls, kids were gawking at him, talking fast, wishing him luck. They seemed jittery, but he felt calm. Loose. *Gimme the ball*, he thought. *I'll sink one at the buzzer.*

Somebody said, "Crank up the old grease gun, Tom," and somebody else said, "Put the Brutzky on his butt and I'll vote for you for anything." A few kids glared at him—maybe they were friends of Britzky—but not too many.

"How does everybody know about it already?"

Alessa held up her telephone. "You send it to a few people and it goes viral."

"Viral? Like a virus—a disease, right?"

Spreading disease by telephone. What was wrong with this planet?

He enjoyed going through the halls with all eyes on him. Game Day. That was kind of like a dream, too. *I miss football. Can't wait for hoops to start.*

A couple of times during the morning, his mind flashed back to last night, to Grandpa, to Homeplace, to the questions he didn't get to ask about Dad. *Grandpa said he raised us to be rebel leaders.* He wondered what Dad would think of his plan.

He pushed it all out of his brain the same way he pushed out everything before a game. *Concentrate, Captain Eddie.* Having something to push out always helped him focus on the game.

"So do you have a plan?" said Alessa.

"About what?"

"C'mon, Tom, stop playing. The showdown's getting closer. The whole school is going to be there. Everybody."

"That's my plan."

FORTY-SIX

BRITZKY was waiting at the fountain, his sleeves rolled up like he was ready to fight.

But his eyes didn't look ready, Eddie thought. He was scared. "Glad you're here, man," Eddie said. "I'm gonna need your help."

Britzky's eyes got buggy. "What're you talking about?"

"I need a bodyguard in case anybody gets a bad idea. I need somebody I can trust to cover my back."

Britzky's mouth fell open. He stared at Eddie. "You trust me?"

"You're on my team, Britzky."

"Todd. My name is Todd."

"I know you can do it, Todd."

Eddie climbed up on the fountain. Hundreds of kids

were there. Teachers, too. It was bigger than any pep rally in his school on EarthTwo. He felt terrific. Like going from the school gym to Madison Square Garden.

He raised his arms. People quieted down.

He thought about Dad, how he would say it. They mostly talked sports, but Dad had loads to say about thinking for yourself and doing the right thing.

"Okay, everybody, listen up. I know you came here to see a fight, but my friend Todd Britzky and I have something more important to do."

Silence.

"We're declaring tomorrow Tech Off! Day.

"Tomorrow, for one day, no phones, computers—any of that stuff. People are going to have to talk to each other."

At first, Eddie could tell, they thought it was a joke. Kids shrugged, screwed up their faces, rolled their eyes. The way their thumbs were going, they must be sending messages to each other. One kid tried to climb up the fountain to take a close-up picture of Eddie with his phone, but Britzky blocked him and stared him down.

"I think we all kind of forgot how to talk face-to-face, work out problems, stuff like that, because we spend so much time pretending we're talking—on the phone, on the Facepage, Tweeter, you know. I'm not saying throw away your cell phones and stuff, I'm just saying take a day off from them. Just one day. Twenty-four hours. Tech Off! Day."

He spotted Alessa looking up from the crowd. Her eyes were a little squinty, as if she was trying to figure out if he was sincere. He looked right at her.

"I got this idea because I couldn't do what everybody else could do on the computer and phone. At first I felt like a total dumbbell. But then I started listening to people while I looked at their faces, and I figured out what they really meant about things. That's why Todd and I are friends instead of enemies."

Britzky turned to look up at Eddie. His eyes were shiny. He thrust a huge fist into the air. "Tom Canty for president!"

The crowd cheered and whistled. They raised their fists. They started shouting, "Tom Canty for president!" until Eddie raised his arms for silence. It took a few minutes.

"That's it. I think everybody should just turn your head to the right and look the nearest person in the eye and shake their hand and say, 'Hi,' and say your name to them. C'mon, even if it feels goofy. Try it."

For a moment, no one moved. Then Merlyn loudly said, "Hi, I'm Merlyn," and laughed and shook Dr.

Traum's hand, and the basketball coach grabbed Mrs. Rupp's hand, and Hannah the green-haired girl grabbed raccoon eyes' hand. It started as goofing around, Eddie could tell, but then teachers and kids got into it, and they started talking about it. Of course they held up their phones and took pictures of shaking each other's hands, but hey, it was a start.

They clapped and cheered as Eddie climbed down. He grabbed Todd's wrist with one hand and Alessa's with the other and held them up for pictures.

Eddie shook Todd's hand. "I'm really sorry about that stink bomb."

"No problem, bro," said Britzky. "You were sticking up for your bud. I'm down with that." It took Eddie a moment to figure out what he meant, but then he thought it was great. He shook Todd's hand again, and then put Todd's and Alessa's hands together until they shook.

Alessa started dragging Eddie away. "This is going to be huge. Maybe you should run for *school* president. For starters."

At the edge of the crowd, they came face-to-face with Dr. Traum. "Very clever, Eddie. That's not something Tom could do."

The good feeling began to drain away. There was a growing cold spot in his gut.

As they walked away, Alessa said, "What was that all about? Why did he call you Eddie?"

Eddie shrugged. "Must have me mixed up with somebody else."

PART THREE

GOOD ENOUGH

FORTY-SEVEN

I RODE Eddie's bike to school, a red Schwinn that han-
dled like a dump truck. No gears. To brake, you had
to push back on the pedals. I should have walked. There
were lots of other bikes in the racks near the fountain,
and none of them were locked up. Didn't they steal bikes
back in the old days—I mean, *these* days? Who would
want these old bikes anyway?

Kids in homeroom were buzzing when I got there. I
wondered if they knew what I knew about what was going to happen today. But how could they?

Ronnie showed up in the same raggedy yellow
sweater-shirt he had on yesterday, even a little dirtier.
He tugged on my sleeve. "Hot skinny, boss. Get set for
duck and cover."

"What's that?"

He shook his head. "Gee, Eddie, you really got conked. I hope you're . . ."

"I'm fine. Duck and cover what?"

"In case the Commies attack. We hide under our desks."

"Why?" I asked.

"Don't you remember? To protect us from the hydrogen bomb. Blast, flash, radioactive fallout."

"Wake up," I said. "We'll fry whatever we do. Everybody knows that."

The way he looked at me, I realized nobody knew that. Except me.

The homeroom teacher clapped her hands. "I don't want anybody bumping their heads. You all know what to do. Wait for the siren."

The classroom loudspeaker crackled, and then a siren screamed.

The teacher yelled, "Duck and cover!"

Everybody dropped down and crawled under a desk. They put their heads down between their knees and their hands over the back of their heads. Even the teacher.

Everybody except me. Merlyn looked up and spotted me sitting up. She yelled, "Eddie's not ducking!"

The teacher popped up from under her desk. "Eddie! Get down!"

"What for? It's silly. The Russians are never going to attack."

"We don't know that," she said.

I know that, but if I tell you how I know, you'll think I'm nuts.

"Please, Eddie." She was begging. "I know you hurt your head, but . . ."

"This is all a big trick to keep us scared and doing what the guys in charge want us to do."

Dad had told me that.

"We can talk about that later, just please do this. For me. It's the law. Nobody wants you to get in trouble."

I didn't move. I said, "I don't do what I'm told if it's stupid." As soon as I said it, I realized that was me—Tom—talking. But I was supposed to be Eddie.

She waited a few minutes until the all-clear siren sounded, and then she marched me down the hall and pointed to a hard wooden bench outside an office with a glass door you couldn't see through. The glass looked like frosty bubbles. There were black letters on the glass: DR. TRAUM, SCHOOL PSYCHOLOGIST.

Dr. Traum? Here? It could be a coincidence. Maybe it's a common name. But Grandpa said that monitors can be in two places at the same time.

The homeroom teacher said, "I have to do this, Eddie.

Rules." She knocked. There was no answer. She knocked again.

"Just wait here, Eddie. I'm sorry." She looked like she was sorry. She walked away with her head down.

It was funny. Teachers loved to turn Tom in, to get him in bigger trouble. They hated to get Eddie in trouble. I wondered what I could get away with here as Eddie.

As soon as she was gone and the coast was clear, I opened Dr. Traum's office door.

It was a boring office, a big dark wooden desk with a wood swivel chair behind it and three hard wood chairs in front. The desk was piled with papers. Bookcases and file cabinets. On the walls were pictures of Mickey Mantle, the Rev. Billy Graham, Vice President Richard Nixon with his dog, Checkers, who looked like Buddy, and Dr. Jonas Salk, the guy who invented the polio vaccine. Dr. Traum was in every picture with his arm around the famous person. Both were smiling. The Dr. Traum in the picture was wearing a suit with wide shoulders and a skinny tie. He didn't have a ponytail. But it was Dr. Traum all right. The pictures looked Photoshopped. *He's a phony on all planets.*

I sat down in Dr. Traum's chair and swiveled around a couple of times. This was too crazy. It had to be a dream. In a moment, I would wake up and hear the Lump eating like a garbage disposal, see Britzky slamming into

Alessa, watch Mrs. Rupp waving her laser beam along her timeline.

I went through Dr. Traum's desk drawers—more papers and envelopes and pens and stuff. In a bottom drawer were a couple of switchblade knives, a slingshot, and brass knuckles he must have taken from students. *Wait another fifty years, Doc, you'll be taking away guns and a TPT GreaseShot IV.*

Fifty years. I checked the calendar behind Dr. Traum's desk. Today was Friday, October 4, 1957.

Today's the day, all right.

Sputnik.

I took a deep breath. I should have been scared, but I wasn't. I felt juiced.

The school's public-address system was on a table next to the desk. It looked like a Playskool setup, a microphone with a wire attached to a box with levers on it. Technology was pretty simple in 1957.

I flipped all the levers up.

"Attention, please. Attention, please. This is . . . um . . . Eddie Tudor speaking. The world is going to change today. The Russians are coming. But not the way you think. It's nothing to be afraid of, but you'd better start learning about science, because the Russians are sending up the first satellite to orbit the Earth. It's called *Sputnik.*"

It was fun. I was trying to think of more things to say when the door burst open. Dr. Traum rushed in and grabbed for the PA switch.

Behind him were the two thugs in white uniforms.

FORTY-EIGHT

I WAS strapped into a straitjacket and pushed into the back of a white van. One of the two thugs kept turning to glare at me. I recognized him. He was the one I'd nailed with the cell phone bomb in Washington Square Park on EarthOne.

"Think you're hot stuff, punk?"

"Hot as pepper spray," I said.

I thought he was going to jump over the seat, but the other guy, who was driving, grabbed his arm. "Let it go, Earl. Doc doesn't want anything happening to the kid until he's done with him."

"Then we get him?"

"Yeah. We'll teach him to be more of a human being."

They both laughed and started talking about snatching the other kid. I figured they meant Eddie. Was there any way to warn him?

We drove for almost an hour on highways and back roads before we came to a high chainlink fence topped with barbed wire. Inside the fence was a large building that looked like a castle, with two gray stone towers and tiny barred windows. The sign on the metal fence read: THE UNION COUNTY HOSPITAL FOR THE CRIMINALLY INSANE.

It was the "snake pit" I'd read about online that had turned into a juvenile jail. I remembered more — a tornado had knocked off one of the towers in 1957. But that hadn't happened yet.

The van pulled up in front of a stone guardhouse, and a man in uniform came out to talk to the driver, whom he called Duke.

I'd read that there was a secret tunnel from the asylum that ran under the fence to the guardhouse. After the tornado, some of the patients managed to get out of their cells and escape through the tunnel. They were recaptured, and they claimed it hadn't been a tornado that knocked off the tower but a spaceship with aliens. No one believed them because . . . well, because they were patients in an insane asylum.

The fence swung open, and the van drove up to the front door. Duke and Earl pulled me out and pushed me inside the building, then down a long dim corridor and into a little concrete cell. They unstrapped the straitjacket.

The door clanged shut.

The cell had a cot and a hole in the floor for a toilet. The window had bars on it, but it was too high to look out of, and I was too tired to try to jump up.

It was still daylight. I stretched out on the bed.

I wondered why I didn't feel scared anymore. I guess I thought it was a dream or a coma after all. Think about it: Two planets. Switching places with my imaginary twin. Going back in time, or at least sideways. You have to be crazy or unconscious. And the two Dr. Traums. Were they twins, too? Even the name sounded phony.

The cell door swung open and one of the Dr. Traums walked in.

"We'll move you to a more comfortable room," he said, "as soon as you let us help you." His voice was soft and friendly.

"What kind of help?"

"Tell me about the voices."

"What voices?"

He sat down on the cot. "What do they tell you to do?"

"They say don't answer stupid questions."

Dr. Traum smiled. "I can understand your being a little, um, miffed, about being dragged here. But it's for your own good."

I kept my mouth shut.

"Eddie Tudor has always been a polite, hard-working, nice young man. But something happened recently to change you. I think it's the voices."

I just stared into his green eyes. I thought I saw my reflection. I had the feeling there were cameras behind those green eyes.

I have to be careful. Anything he gets out of me could make trouble for my brother and my grandfather.

"What voices?" I said.

"Do you ever hear from your father?"

"My dad disappeared two years ago."

"All the more reason to want to hear from him."

"I never heard from him."

"I believe you," said Dr. Traum. "He'd be much too clever for that—and selfish, allowing you to believe he was dead."

"You're saying he's *not* dead?"

He smiled. "Tell me, when did you first start imagining you had a twin brother?"

"What twin brother?"

"The one on another planet, the one you talked to in your backyard."

"Where did you hear that?"

Dr. Traum smiled. "Typical Tom, the smart, bad one." He leaned against the wall. "Have you talked to Eddie lately? Do you know where he is, if he's all right?"

"I'm Eddie."

"Actually, Eddie will be here in a little while, and if you don't tell me what I want to know, then *he'll* tell me. And we won't need you anymore."

I tried hard to keep my face still as a stone. I'd seen plenty of TV shows where bad guys used this kind of interrogation trick. But my mind was in high gear. Dad alive? Eddie coming here? Had they captured him, too?

"Eddie is concerned about you. He wants to help me help you."

"If he's imaginary, how can he come here?"

"Eddie can come here because he's you, the other part of your personality. You'll imagine him here."

He was trying to confuse me.

"I know this seems confusing."

Was he reading my thoughts or was he trying to put thoughts in my head? "Maybe I'm imagining you," I said.

He nodded and smiled more. "That's clever, Tom, just like your father."

"What about my dad?"

"What about him?" said Dr. Traum.

"Did you know him?"

"If you let me help you, we could talk about your dad."

Careful. He's getting very tricky.

193

"Help me how?" I said.

"Help you become as terrific a boy as I know you can be. I want to help you get free from that story your mind created about a twin brother and aliens."

Aliens. Had I ever mentioned aliens to him? Had I talked about them to anyone besides Grandpa and Eddie? *Be very careful, Tom.*

"What about aliens?"

Dr. Traum's smile disappeared. "Don't play with me, Thomas. We're going to have all of you very soon. No one will get hurt if you cooperate. Where's your father?"

"He disappeared two years ago."

Dr. Traum's face got very cold. The green eyes glowed hot. "Don't lie to me, or I'll leave you in this place to rot. When did you last hear from your father?"

"Two years ago."

"Not as human as he pretends to be, is he? For two years he let you think he was dead."

My stomach turned over. "He *is* alive!"

Dr. Traum stalked out.

After the door slammed shut, I tore the sheet on the cot into three long strips, tied them together, and knotted one end. It took me a while to throw the knot around one of the bars and pull myself up to the window. I searched the sky for the blinking lights. It was hard hanging on to the bars. Nothing. I tried to throw my thoughts up there.

Hear me, Eddie! I'm in an insane asylum. I need help. Tell Grandpa the aliens got me. And they're coming after you. And Dad's alive!

After a while, I lost my grip and fell. I was cold and hungry and scared. It was hard to block out the constant noise of inmates screaming and banging their tin cups against the bars. I started to cry. I couldn't help myself.

There was a slot at the bottom of the cell door with a hinged flap, like a doggy door, and someone slid a tray in. A tuna fish sandwich, a tin cup of milk, and a dish of green Jell-O. I was hungry, but I didn't eat or drink anything. What if there were drugs in there—like a truth serum—to get me talking?

But I didn't know anything.

Eddie! Talk to me!

FORTY-NINE

NEW YORK CITY
2011

Eddie enjoyed the limo ride into Manhattan. A TV show was playing on a screen on the back seat. Amazing. There was a cabinet filled with candy, cookies, and bottles of soda and water. There were four different kinds of water. He couldn't remember water in fancy bottles on EarthTwo. You filled your canteen if you were going to need water on a hike or for a day of playing ball outside.

"You look pretty relaxed," said Alessa. She and Britzky were sucking down water between cookies. "Want to practice?"

"Sure."

Alessa opened her notebook. "The big question they sent is, Why did you start this campaign and what do you hope is the takeaway?"

"The takeaway?"

She sighed. "What people think about and do because of it."

"Just shut down for a day and talk to each other."

"And after that?" She sounded like one of those patient teachers talking to a special ed kid. She was trying
to coach him. He realized how much he liked her, his
first friend who was a girl.

Eddie shrugged. "I don't know."

"You might say, If people start talking, maybe they'll
get along better," said Alessa. "It could lead to all kinds
of good things. Like world peace."

"Cool," said Eddie.

Britzky said, "What if they show the YouTube clip of
Tom greasing that dude in his other school? That's not
world peace."

Alessa raised her eyebrows at Britzky. "Good catch,
Todd. Tom can say he's changed and that means we can
all change. Don't mention the pills."

"What pills?" said Eddie. He had forgotten about
them.

Alessa stared at him. "OMG. You haven't forgotten
them, too, have you? Are you still taking them?"

Whoops. "LOL."

Alessa clapped her hands. "You're ready, Tom. This is
going to be so fun."

It was. It went by in a blur. Smiley young women

hurried Eddie through the halls and into a room where an older woman powdered his face and combed his hair and then into a studio where a woman who looked like Alessa's mom sat facing him in a chair under hot lights. They were talking for a few minutes before Eddie realized that they were on television.

"People your age are supposed to be addicted to electronics," said the woman. "So, Tom Canty, what was it that made you so different?"

"People at my school weren't talking to each other. They weren't working out their problems," said Eddie.

"Was there one event that gave you this idea?"

"I was supposed to have a fight with this kid I didn't even know, and he didn't know me. He sent me texts challenging me. When we got face-to-face and started talking, we became friends." Even as he said it, Eddie knew it wasn't exactly true, but the look on her face —she was loving it!—pushed him on. And wasn't this what Tom would say? "I think countries could do that."

"'Countries could do that.' Tom, that is such a profound statement."

He didn't remember what else they talked about, but she hugged him, and so did all the smiley young women in the hallway. The lady who rubbed off his makeup gave him a kiss.

"Great job," said Alessa.

Britzky was banging on his shoulder.

"Thanks for coaching me, guys. Couldn't have done it without you."

Outside on the street, there were a dozen people asking for his autograph.

"Maybe you should be running for president of the country," said Alessa.

"Do you have to be a certain age?" asked Britzky. "I know you have to be born in America."

"I was born in America," said Eddie. *Just on another planet.*

FIFTY

THE limo dropped them off at school. The banner was hanging from the front door: TECH OFF! DAY AT NEARMONT MIDDLE SCHOOL.

"I wonder what Tom would think," said Eddie before he realized he was talking out loud.

"The old Tom would have hated it," said Alessa. "But you really like it, don't you?"

"Yeah."

At lunch, kids and teachers came over to touch him and talk to him. The attention was almost as good as football, Eddie thought.

Mrs. Rupp smiled as he sat down in her class. "We might just have to add a date on the timeline for you, Thomas."

Dr. Traum grabbed him on the way out of class and

steered him into his office. "You made us all proud, Thomas. You were just so natural, so relaxed." His big green eyes seemed to be glowing.

Watch out.

"Was this Tech Off! Day all your idea?" Dr. Traum asked.

"Alessa thought it would help my campaign to be class president."

Dr. Traum smiled. "Sounds like twenty-first-century politics to me. Although it does seem like such a change for you. You've always been such a wired, electronic-gadgets kind of guy."

Eddie shrugged.

"A remarkable change. A few days ago, people would have said that Tom Canty was a disruptive, uncooperative, unhappy boy. And now he's a polite, hard-working, nice young man."

"Isn't that a good thing?" Eddie stayed calm. He could tell from the way Dr. Traum leaned away from him while smiling that he was up to something. A quarterback is always studying his opponents' body language. It was like reading a linebacker about to attack. *Don't forget he called you Eddie yesterday.*

"Of course. But any sudden change is a reason to wonder. Often it happens when someone . . . oh, for example, begins hearing voices. You may think they are, perhaps, aliens from some other planet, but they are from inside you."

"Aliens?"

"Enjoy your day, Tom. Now back to class."

It was a good day even if Dr. Traum had made him nervous. That must have been his plan. *He's trying to get me off my game*, Eddie thought. *Think of something else, something positive.*

In gym, he had something great to think about — the basketball season! He worked out with some of the kids who would be on the team. That was really neat, being the only seventh-grader. He was much better than most of them. Some were flashier players, with no-look passes and fancy crossover dribbles, but Eddie had no trouble keeping up with them on breakaways and slashing through to the basket. They couldn't stop his jumper.

The guys were nice, and the coach winked and told him that he'd be getting a number soon. Eddie liked the idea of playing here, although he wished the uniforms weren't so long and baggy. He was going to miss those nice tight satiny shorts he wore on EarthTwo.

Keith was waiting for him at home with pizza and an ice cream cake. He'd seen *The Today Show*. "Great job," he said.

They talked to Tom's mom on Keith's laptop computer. Her face appeared on the screen! She had seen *The Today Show* in Dallas. She thought he looked terrific, fit and muscular. And his hair looked shorter. Keith broke in to tell her that *The Ellen Show* had called. If they flew out to Los Angeles to do the show, they could meet up. It was jolly. Tom's mom was pretty and seemed nice.

They watched the Yankees game for a while. Eddie started nodding and Keith sent him up to bed, but he couldn't fall asleep. He began feeling cold, hungry, and scared. He burrowed under the covers, wishing Buddy was there with him.

He wondered if Tom was in trouble. He couldn't understand feeling so bad after such a great day.

He waited until he heard Keith come upstairs and close his bedroom door before he got dressed again and sneaked downstairs and out into the backyard. He looked for the blinking lights. Nothing. *Maybe you don't need them here.* He concentrated as hard as he could. *Can you hear me, Tom? What's going on? Are you okay?*

He thought he heard Tom say something about being in an insane asylum . . . he needed help . . . tell Grandpa. But it sounded like a distant echo deep inside his head. The words rattled around. Maybe it was his imagination. Maybe it was those voices Dr. Traum was talking about.

I could be going crazy.

But I have to do something.

Get to Grandpa.

He was so busy finding the light switch on Tom's fancy bike that he didn't notice the white van parked at the curb until the doors flew open and two big men in white uniforms jumped out.

One of them pulled out a small can and sprayed a sour-smelling liquid in Eddie's face.

"See how *you* like it, punk," he said.

"This is the other one, Earl."

The last thing Eddie remembered was feeling sorry that he had left Tom's bike lying in the middle of the driveway.

FIFTY-ONE

IN what seemed like a dream, Eddie was heading back to EarthTwo, hungry, thirsty, wracked by the flu-like symptoms of slipping. The sour spray smell was in his nose and throat. When he woke up, he was sitting against a tree.

It hadn't been a dream. The two big men in white uniforms who had grabbed him outside Tom's house now took his arms and dragged him into a white van. One of them handed him a canteen of water. Eddie guzzled it.

"Easy, fella. Too much'll make you sick." The man pulled the canteen away.

"Let him get sick," said the other one.

"I told you, Earl, this ain't the kid from the park, the pepper spray punk."

"I don't like either of 'em, Duke."

They drove for a while. A high chainlink fence with

barbed wire on top loomed up, beyond it a gray castle with towers.

They pulled Eddie out of the van and supported him up the stairs to the front door. His legs were wobbly. They hustled him down a corridor and into a small concrete room with a cot and a toilet hole. The window had bars on it, but it was too high to look out.

"Welcome, Eddie."

It was Dr. Traum. Smiling. Leaning away from him.

Concentrate, stay calm.

"Where am I?"

"In a place where we can help you."

"Help me?"

"Help you with the voices, with the strange feelings. Were you feeling sick?"

"Yeah."

"And now you're better."

"What's going to happen?"

"That all depends on you, Eddie."

"What do you mean?"

"The voices, Eddie. Your brother. Your father."

Careful. He swallowed down the excitement coming up into his chest. "What about them?"

Dr. Traum stood up. "We'll talk again. I'll send you some food."

Moments after he slammed the cell door, the doggy

door opened and a tray slid in. A tuna fish sandwich, a tin cup of milk, a dish of green Jell-O.

Eddie wolfed it all down, too fast. The food became a ball in the pit of his stomach. He stretched out on the cot. He was exhausted. His head felt like a rattle, pieces of sounds and words tumbling inside, scraping and clattering against the inside of his skull. Tom was in there, calling to him.

Eddie—you there, Eddie?

The voices again.

He tried to shut them down, slow the rattle, think, but Tom's voice got louder.

I'm right here, Eddie.

The voices got lost in the screaming of inmates and the rattling of tin cups against cell bars. Eddie remembered how he could shut out the crowd noise when he needed to focus to throw a pass, sink a free throw, pitch out of a jam. He could imagine narrowing his brain to keep everything out. *Find something to concentrate on,* he told himself.

He thought of Buddy, wagging his stub of a tail, licking his face.

I'm in the insane asylum, Eddie. In the cell next door.

FIFTY-TWO

WHEN Tom didn't get on the school bus, Alessa almost got off. She felt nervous without him. Kids were looking at her. As usual, she wondered if they were making comments about her size and what she was wearing. She ordered herself to toughen up. *They're not talking about you, Lessi. They're still talking about Tech Off! Day.*

It had been extended for a second day. She missed using her phone. She felt lonely. Her thumbs twitched. She remembered when she used to suck them not that long ago, just before she got her first smartphone.

Then Britzky walked up the aisle and leaned over the seat in front of her. His breath smelled of garbage. What did he eat for breakfast? She lifted up her backpack as a shield.

"Where's Tom?" he asked.

It was almost a whine, she thought. He looked worried. Being Tom's bodyguard must be such a big deal for him. *You're not better than him, Lessi. Being Tom's friend and adviser is such a big deal for you.*

She couldn't believe she was trying to understand Britzky. She'd never thought of him as having any human feelings. *Maybe he feels like an outsider, too.* Tom had figured that out—the new Tom, the nicer, people-person Tom. But she did miss the old Tom's smartness, and his violin playing.

"I don't know," said Alessa. "I haven't heard from him."

"I guess he wouldn't answer his cell on a Tech Off! Day."

"He doesn't have one."

"Duh." Britzky rapped his skull. It was kind of cute for a brute. "I shoulda thought of that."

"If I hear anything, I'll let you know. What's your number?"

He didn't remember. He had to pull out his phone.

Nobody ever calls him, she thought.

"Hey, thanks," he said. He smiled at her. It came out crooked, like he wasn't used to smiling.

"No problem." She thought for a second. " . . . Todd."

He widened the smile, uncrooking it.

She could tell he really liked being called Todd. *Oh, you got some moves, girl.*

People *were* looking at her in school, she decided, but it was all right. She was Tom's friend. A few people even asked her where he was, and she tried to be mysterious about it, not letting on that she didn't know, either. Teachers were talking about Tech Off! Day in their classes, and there were arguments, but not nasty arguments—more like friendly discussions, like whether this was a good idea or not. Some kids wondered if people secretly didn't want to talk to each other and that was why texting was so popular, and then some political kids said that maybe Google and Apple and Verizon and those other companies were pushing this stuff down our throats just to make money and we shouldn't let them get away with it.

It was interesting. It wasn't that everyone was for it or against it or there was a big split in the school like color war at camp. And kids *were* cheating; she spotted a few thumbs in action. But people were actually having conversations. Alessa felt proud that she was part of it. But she wished Tom were there. Where could he be?

There was an assembly to celebrate how special Nearmont was to have the first Tech Off! Day. A woman from Apple, the company that made the school's computers, said that Apple supported Tech Off! Day because it gave people a chance to appreciate how important technology was on all their other days. Apple was going to give the school ten of its latest Macs.

The teachers led the applause. Britzky leaned over and said, "That doesn't make sense."

Alessa was about to say, "You're not as dumb as you look," but she bit her tongue. He might not take that right.

Mrs. Rupp didn't use her PowerPoint in history. She was still planning to add the first Tech Off! Day to her timeline.

There was more noise than usual in the cafeteria. Alessa wondered whether that was because kids were actually talking to each other or because of the excitement over having all the cameras and reporters.

Britzky, sitting at her table, said, "Where's Tom?" for the fourth time. Alessa thought he was like a dog waiting for his master to come home.

"On another planet," Alessa snapped. She hated to keep admitting she didn't know.

"Yeah . . . I always thought he was from another planet," said Hannah, the girl with green hair.

"Both of them," said the boy with the raccoon eyes.

"Both?" said Alessa and Britzky together.

"He changed," said raccoon eyes. "He was like two totally different people."

"The pills," said Alessa.

"He really was like two different people," said Britzky. "He got super nice. He made you want to be his friend."

"He got boring," said raccoon eyes.

Kids kept coming over looking for Tom. The basketball coach asked where he was. One of the jocks swaggered over, and Britzky jumped up, his arms crossed on his chest, standing between the jock and Alessa. *Now he's bodyguarding me,* Alessa thought. *This is too weird.* But she liked it. The jock just wanted to say that the basketball team was behind Tom's campaign.

"I'll tell him," said Alessa. "Thanks." Cool the way people were looking at her like she was somebody.

But a somebody would do *something.*

Late in the day, she did something. She ditched gym and locked herself in a stall in the girls' bathroom. She made sure her phone was on vibrate when she turned it on to check for messages. *Please let there be something from Tom.*

Nothing.

She needed to talk to somebody. She waited in the hall until Britzky came out of the gym.

"Todd? Do you think something could have happened to Tom?"

"Like what?"

"I don't know. It's as if he just disappeared off the face of the earth."

Britzky lowered his voice. "Alien abduction."

"Do you believe in stuff like that?"

He looked a little embarrassed, but he nodded his head.

"You think something is going on here? In school?"

"Everywhere. You can feel it."

Alessa looked at him carefully. "When do you feel it?"

He leaned closer. Alessa could see cheese between his teeth. He whispered, "With Tom."

She jerked back. "Like what?"

He shrugged. "I get a feeling when I'm around him. It's like a hum. Maybe a buzz."

Alessa felt a quivery chill rising up to her chest. "Me, too." She took a chance. "I think something bad is going on. He might be in trouble."

Britzky's eyes looked fiery. "What can we do?"

"Dr. Traum. Maybe he could help us."

"Do you trust him?" said Britzky.

"No. But who else is there?"

FIFTY-THREE

RONNIE was hungry. Half of Eddie's huge lunch sandwich was usually Ronnie's major meal of the day. And Ronnie was lonely. Eddie was the only kid in school who let him hang around. Early in the morning, waiting for the food deliveries for the cafeteria, he spotted Dr. Traum in the parking lot and ran over to him.

"Dr. Traum, I've got some news about Eddie."

"Do you." His glittering green eyes made Ronnie feel chilly all over.

It took him a moment to remember what he had dreamed up to say. "Remember when you asked me about voices? Well, Eddie thinks his dog is talking to him."

"Does he, now."

It wasn't working. Dr. Traum wasn't interested, Ronnie thought. *Could he tell I was lying, or does he know where Eddie is? Take a chance.*

"Where's Eddie?" he asked Dr. Traum.

"In a safe place."

"Where's that?"

"I'm in a hurry, Ronnie." Dr. Traum pulled his briefcase out of his black Cadillac, slammed the door, and rushed off. He was inside the school before Ronnie noticed that he had left his keys in the ignition.

By the time Ronnie got back to the rear of the building, the delivery men had finished unloading the food and locked it inside the school. Ronnie had no chance to swipe even a can of mixed fruit, his favorite.

He trudged back to Dr. Traum's car, opened the door, and pulled the keys out of the ignition. He would take them to Dr. Traum. Maybe then Dr. Traum would tell him about Eddie.

He noticed a pile of coins in the ashtray: enough to get breakfast at the diner. Boy, was he hungry. He scooped out the change and dropped it into his pocket with the keys. It would be a loan. He'd tell Dr. Traum. He locked the black Cadillac. He thought it was a pretty fancy car.

Even so, he felt a little guilty eating the egg sandwich he bought with Dr. Traum's change. But it tasted so good and filled his stomach.

Without Eddie around, the day dragged for Ronnie. Three times he went to the psychologist's office to turn in the car keys, but Dr. Traum was never there. Ronnie didn't want to just leave them. He wanted to trade them for some information about Eddie.

After school he went to the County Recreation Center, where he could take a shower and eat leftovers from the senior lunch program in exchange for helping the janitor set up chairs for the evening meetings.

At dusk it was time to think about a place to sleep. He didn't want to go back to the church where he had hidden his bag of clothes. The priest had spotted him last time and invited him in for a meal, but the guy had seemed creepy. The railroad cops were checking out the boxcars more regularly, and the regular cops were running more patrols around the summer houses on the lake because there had been a few burglaries.

He remembered Dr. Traum's fancy car. It should be comfortable.

It was still there. He unlocked it, put the keys back into the ignition, and crawled under some blankets in the back. Dr. Traum had said Eddie was in a safe place. He wondered if Eddie was at the Union County asylum. It was somewhere out in the country. The weekend he'd been there had been awful, in a cold little cell with a hole for a toilet. He got a headache from the constant noise, the patients screaming and banging their tin cups against the bars. They let him go when his caseworker showed up with a new foster mom. Why would Eddie be there?

Eddie was different these days since he fell at Boy Scout camp. He looked thinner. He talked faster. And the violin—where did *that* come from? Eddie had never said he could play. *How could he keep something like that from me, his sidekick?*

Ronnie fell asleep.

When he woke up, the car was moving.

FIFTY-FOUR

NEARMONT, N.J.
2011

THE door to Dr. Traum's office was closed, but Alessa and Britzky could see a light through the pebbly glass. They heard low voices. They sat down on the bench in the hall to wait.

"What are we going to say to him?" asked Britzky.

"Tell him everything we think."

"He'll think we're nuts."

"He's not like that," said Alessa. "He's very sympathetic."

"How do you know?"

"From orchestra. And he cares about Tom, too."

"But maybe he's not into paranormal stuff," said Britzky.

"He's a psychologist—he'll listen to us."

"About alien abduction and replacement?"

"Replacement?" said Alessa.

"Tom is suddenly different, right? He turns nice, he gets people to like him, he's a great basketball player. Alien replacement is a big deal."

"I hadn't thought of that." Alessa felt a shiver of excitement.

Britzky's face was getting redder. "There's too much stuff you can't explain any other way. And the government doesn't want us to find out about it."

"Why not? So we don't freak out?"

"No, so they can make deals. If, like, China makes friends with the aliens before we do, we're toast."

Alessa rocked back. She hadn't thought of that, either. "You think Tom is an alien?"

Britzky shrugged. "Or is under some kind of alien mind control."

"You just think of that?"

Britzky shook his head. "I think about this stuff all the time."

She wanted to grab Britzky's arm. "You think Tom could be in trouble?"

"Trouble?" said Dr. Traum. They hadn't heard his door open. He was smiling. "I'm sure we can work it out together. Come in."

Alessa glanced at Britzky. He looked as nervous as she felt. Something wasn't right.

Dr. Traum closed the door behind them and said,

"The young heroes are here, Merlyn, straight from the pages of Marvel comics."

Merlyn was sitting in Dr. Traum's swivel chair, laughing.

What's she doing here? Alessa thought.

"Actually, Traum," said Merlyn, "it's not comics—it's computer-generated images from Pixar. You need to keep up with the times."

"I'll leave that to you. These times disgust me," said Dr. Traum.

Merlyn reached into her backpack and pulled out a spray can. Alessa wondered if it was some kind of beauty product.

Britzky yelled, "Look out!" but Merlyn was already spraying a sour-smelling liquid in their faces.

FIFTY-FIVE

THE UNION COUNTY (N.J.) HOSPITAL
FOR THE CRIMINALLY INSANE
1957

ONNIE was afraid to move. The dust on the blanket tickled his nose. He held his nose between his thumb and forefinger so he wouldn't sneeze. He tried to breathe softly through his mouth.

Dr. Traum was talking. "Traum here. I am driving back to the asylum. You can bring the station down as planned."

Who could he be talking to? Ronnie wondered.

"The boy and the girl are on their way from EarthOne with Merlyn. I don't think the twins know where their father is. But I'm convinced he'll try to save them or give himself up for them. He was always a little too human. End for now."

Something clicked, as if Dr. Traum had turned off a switch.

Ronnie burrowed deeper into the blanket. The car

was moving fast, so they must be on a highway. *To where? What boy and girl? What twins? What does Merlyn have to do with this?*

After a while, the car stopped, and Dr. Traum had a quick conversation with someone. Ronnie could hear the scrape of metal, as if a steel fence was sliding open. The car started up again.

There was a click. "Traum again. I'm sending Earl back to the school to pick up Ronnie. Should have thought of it earlier. The little mouse is harmless, but we should have everyone involved in custody before we proceed. End for now."

Click.

The car stopped again. This time, Dr. Traum shut off the engine and got out. Ronnie counted to a hundred before he carefully crawled out from under the blanket and peeked through the window.

It was night. He could dimly see a big gray building with towers. It was surrounded by a high chainlink fence. Beyond it was nothing but vacant lots and what looked like factories in the distance.

We're back at the asylum, all right.

"The little mouse is harmless." Ronnie felt anger bubble up in his stomach. *I'm stupid, too. How could I have believed Dr. Traum, that I was helping him help Eddie?*

He peered over the front seat. The keys were still in the ignition.

If Dr. Traum was that careless, he might just think he left them somewhere.

Maybe I'm not so harmless.

Ronnie climbed onto the front seat and pulled the keys out of the ignition. He pushed them deep into his left pants pocket—the one that didn't have a hole in it. He opened the front door as quietly as he could and slid down into the parking lot. He pushed the door mostly closed without slamming it.

Staying low, he crept to the edge of the asylum. The windows were barred and high off the ground. He circled the building twice before he saw light through a window. He found stones to make a pile high enough so he could peek in. It looked like the cell in which he had spent that awful weekend.

Eddie was in there talking to a guy.

When the guy turned around, he was Eddie, too.

FIFTY-SIX

EDDIE was happy to see Tom until he got a good look at him. Tom's face was pale and sweaty. He was shaking all over. Earl had pushed him into the cell with a laugh and slammed the door so hard, the clanging echoes rattled Eddie's brain. It felt like another football hit.

Eddie hugged his brother. "Are you okay?"

"We're in trouble," said Tom. He slumped into a corner and slid down the wall. He was clutching his backpack like a teddy bear.

"That's a big tickle." Eddie gave the little laugh he used when the team was behind and needed a boost. "We're together now. We'll come up with a way to win."

Tom shook his head slowly. "We can't win. The monitors got us. But Dad is alive. He must be in hiding."

"How do you know?"

"Dr. Traum said so."

"Like we trust that creep?" said Eddie.

"He'd have no reason to say it if it wasn't true," said Tom. "He's using us to find him."

"Why?"

"Because Dad's one of the good guys," said Tom. "He's a rebel leader out to defeat the aliens."

"Captain John." Eddie was grinning.

"What?"

"Okay," said Eddie. "We need to get out of here. Up and at 'em." He pulled Tom to his feet.

"What are you doing?" said Tom.

"I've got a plan." Eddie was bouncing a pink rubber ball. "I'm gonna get Duke in a game of Chinese handball. You can sneak out and get help."

Tom said, "That's stupid. How am I gonna get past Duke? And where am I going to go for help?"

"Don't think so much—just do it," said Eddie. "Did you bring that invisibility thing you showed me?"

"The CloakII? It's never worked for me. And even if it does, it only works for about five seconds."

"That's plenty of time," said Eddie. "Once I scored four points in five seconds, a jumper and two free throws."

"This isn't a game, Eddie. And even if I get out, where do I go? I don't know where we are."

"Coach always says, 'When the going gets tough, the tough get going.'"

"That's dumb jock stuff," said Tom.

"You're smart and tough, Tommy. I know you can do it." Eddie began bouncing the ball against the stone wall. "I know you don't want to just sit there and cry."

"I'm not crying."

"Then just do it. The team's counting on you. Must be something."

Tom took a deep breath. There *was* something.

"There's going to be a tornado, but not really. I read about it online."

"When will it happen?" asked Eddie.

"I don't know. Soon, if we're lucky. The patients were right, it *was* a spaceship, not a tornado. And there's a hidden tunnel here somewhere. I read that, too."

"I knew you'd come up with something, Tombo," said Eddie. "Let's go for it."

FIFTY-SEVEN

BRITZKY was scared, but watching Alessa try hard not to show how scared she was made him feel braver. The two of them sat in opposite corners of the cell, which was so small that their feet touched when they stretched their legs out. He let the bottom of his shoes touch hers, as if by accident. She didn't pull hers away.

The sandwiches tasted like paper, and the milk was starting to turn sour, but they finished everything. Even the green Jell-O. Britzky's sick and dizzy feelings were gone, but he could tell that Alessa was exhausted. *She needs my help.*

"Where do you think we are?" said Britzky, for something to say.

"Abducted by aliens makes as much sense as anything else," she said. "But why would they want *us*?"

He didn't want to scare her, but it made him feel

tough to say, "You kidding? Suck out our brains, steal our blood, send us back with pods. Loads of reasons."

It didn't scare her. "Where do you get stuff like that?"

"Mindblender.com. It's the best site for alien intel."

"Intel?"

"Intelligence." He felt good, on a roll. "The government's been keeping all this stuff a big secret."

"Sounds paranoid," said Alessa.

"You're not as dumb as you look, Todd," said Dr. Traum.

Britzky turned so fast he banged his head against the wall. The cell door was open and Dr. Traum was standing in the doorway. "Actually, I've never liked that word, *alien*. It marks people as not belonging. Who is to say who belongs and who doesn't?"

"What are you going to do to us?" said Britzky, trying to keep his voice steady.

Dr. Traum waved his question away. "Talk to me about Tom. Did he ever mention his father?"

"His father disappeared two years ago," said Alessa, "in a plane crash."

"Don't tell him anything," said Britzky.

"Did Tom ever think he heard voices? His father's voice?"

"Tom's not crazy," said Britzky. He liked the way Alessa looked at him, scared but admiring.

"You're right," said Dr. Traum. "Tom's not crazy."

His voice was soft, almost gentle, Britzky thought. *Stay sharp.*

"Tom doesn't know the truth about his father, who is the most dangerous man in the universe. If we don't find John Canty in time, we may not be able to save the planet."

"From who?" asked Britzky.

"Who's 'we'?" asked Alessa.

"I'm hoping you can persuade Tom to tell us what he knows," said Dr. Traum.

"He's here?" said Alessa.

"He's here with his twin brother."

"Twin brother?" they both said.

FIFTY-EIGHT

Sitting between the twins on the cell floor, Alessa felt small and useless. She was surprised that she didn't like feeling small. She had gone back and forth so many times between feeling scared and feeling excited that now she was exhausted. She looked from one twin to the other. They were dressed alike — wrinkled dirty blue shirts and chino pants — but if you looked hard enough, you could see differences.

The one on her left sat up straighter and filled out his shirt. Bigger muscles. The skin on his face was tanner, as if he spent more time outdoors. There was a tiny white scar above his right eyebrow. His hair was shorter. He spoke a little more slowly. He was the nicer one, the basketball player, the one running for class president, the one who had come up with Tech Off! Day.

The one on her right — the thinner and paler one —

talked faster and tougher. He was the Tom she had met first, the one who had been on YouTube, who had bombed Britzky, the violinist, the smarter one.

She wondered which one she liked better. Why was she thinking that? *What's going on?*

"What's going on?" she said.

The twin on her left said, "I'm Eddie. I'm sorry I lied to you, and . . ."

"C'mon, Eddie," snapped the twin on her right. "Just answer her question—if you know the answer."

"Tom!" said Alessa. "Now, you cut that out. We need to work together here."

Tom's mouth shut.

Alessa was surprised and a little thrilled at her power. Britzky gave her a wink. "Go on, Eddie," she said.

"Dr. Traum is an alien," said Eddie. "He thinks we know where our dad is. Dad's a rebel leader against the monitors, which is what the aliens call their scouts on Earth."

"Wow," said Britzky. His eyes were wide. "I knew it. I knew it! Is your dad an alien, too?"

Alessa thought Britzky had never looked so happy.

"Yeah," said Eddie. "Dad quit the monitors when the alien scientists started talking about destroying the Earths."

"How do you know that?" said Tom.

Eddie said, "Grandpa told me."

"He didn't tell *me*."

"You wouldn't have believed him," said Eddie. "On your planet he's supposed to be senile."

"Wait a minute," said Alessa. "You said *Earths*. Are you guys from different planets?"

"There are two Earths," said Tom. "One is in 1957, where we are right now, and the other is in 2011."

Britzky rocked back against the stone wall. "This is *so* cool. Are you guys aliens, too?"

"Half alien," said Eddie. "Our mom was a human. She died when we were born."

The cell door opened, and Dr. Traum walked in, followed by Duke, who stood in the doorway with his arms crossed.

"It's time, people. In a little while, our station ship will be touching down. If we don't have John Canty by then, you'll all be coming back to Homeplace," he said.

"Your planet?" said Britzky.

"Excellent," said Dr. Traum. "You know, I was always under the impression that you were challenged."

Eddie said, "If you haven't caught Dad so far, what makes you think you'll get him now?"

"Us," said Tom. "We're the trap. They expect Dad will come to save us."

Dr. Traum nodded. "We're counting on it. He knows

it would be much better for you if we settle this all here and now, so you can go back to your lives."

Alessa said, "How can you let us go? Aren't you afraid we'll tell everybody?"

"Who would believe you?" said Dr. Traum. "You'd end up here for the rest of your lives, with the rest of the insane. You'd better hope John Canty does the right thing. If we have to take you to Homeplace, you may never see your own homes again."

"What's Homeplace like?" said Britzky.

Alessa thought he sounded interested.

Dr. Traum ignored him. "Duke, call me if anyone remembers anything about John Canty. I'm going out to wait for the station ship."

"Sure. Where's Earl?"

"He's picking up the fifth member of" — Dr. Traum chuckled — "the seventh grade version of those cartoon heroes, the Justice League of America."

FIFTY-NINE

ONCE Dr. Traum was gone, Eddie winked at Tom over his shoulder.

Get ready to disappear.

He began bouncing his pink rubber ball against a wall of the cell.

"I know that game," said Duke. "Ace-King-Queen."

"We call it Chinese handball," said Eddie.

"Why?"

Eddie shrugged. "That's its name. Wanna play?"

Duke looked around. "I'm supposed to be guarding you guys."

"It's not like there's anyplace to go," said Tom.

"Yeah." Duke grinned. "Let's see the ball."

Eddie flipped it to him. Duke bounced it hard. "Good rubber."

"There's not enough room to have a real game with

all of us in here," said Eddie. "Let the rest of them go out in the hall."

"Forget it," said Duke.

"In a real game I'll beat your can blue," said Eddie.

"In your dreams," said Duke.

"Believe it," said Eddie. "I'm going to win. Big."

"Duke's chicken," said Britzky. He flapped his arms and squawked.

"Duke can't think for himself," said Alessa. "Better call Dr. Traum, Dukey, ask him what you should do."

"We can play out in the hall," Duke said to Eddie. He jabbed a finger at Tom, Alessa, and Britzky. "Don't move. Stay where I can see you."

The game started slowly, Duke serving to Eddie against the concrete wall outside the cell.

Tom had never seen Eddie in action before. His brother was quick and graceful, moving to the ball as it bounced off the wall, his feet skipping sideways or backwards, his body curling over, his arm swinging his hand like a paddle to slap the ball back. *How did he get so good?* Tom wondered. *We're twins. I've never been good at sports . . . Maybe because I never tried.*

"Start cheering," whispered Tom to Alessa and Britzky. "Loud."

Duke was grunting and sweating just to keep up with Eddie, who wasn't even breathing hard. Tom realized that Eddie kept placing the ball so that Duke had to run and stretch to get to it. *He's trying to make Duke concentrate on the game and forget about me.*

Tom started edging toward his backpack. He signaled Britzky and Alessa to make more noise, jump around.

"Go for it, big guy!" yelled Britzky. "Nail it."

Alessa stuck her pinkies into her mouth and whistled.

They waved their arms. Stomped. Patients in other cells howled louder and banged their tin cups against the bars.

Eddie slapped a hard shot that Duke was barely able to return, then began hitting little baby shots that had Duke bending over, huffing and puffing. Eddie hit a weak shot that Duke was able to slam back hard. Eddie, apparently off balance, banged it so far out of bounds that Duke had to run down the hall to get it.

Eddie glanced over his shoulder.

Go, Tomaroon.

Tom grabbed his backpack.

Alessa and Britzky were screaming and dancing. The patients were howling and banging.

Tom found the CloakII and turned it on. The power indicator light went from green to yellow.

SIXTY

ABREEZE encircled me. I could feel the light waves being distorted. I couldn't see my feet. It was working! But I had only a few seconds. I tiptoed past Alessa and Britzky, out of the cell, then into the hall, past Eddie, and down the stairs.

The power indicator turned red, then blinked off. My feet reappeared. *Whew. Just made it.*

I was on the ground floor of the asylum. I trotted along a dim hallway toward a barred glass door that looked as though it opened to the outside. I wondered if it would be locked, if there would be an alarm.

Where's the tunnel?

I spotted a green door marked AUTHORIZED PERSON-NEL ONLY. It was locked.

It took the TPT SafecrackerPlus about two seconds to pick the lock. *What do you expect*, I thought. *2011 against 1957.*

The door opened into darkness. I turned on my cell phone flashlight.

I was in a small machinery room. There was a trap-door in the floor. I pulled it open. A ladder led down to a dirt floor. I climbed down. The ceiling there was high enough for me to stand up. It was a tunnel. It had to be the tunnel to the guardhouse.

Go back and get the others. But then what? Could the four of us take Duke?

I started back up the ladder.

The trapdoor slammed shut.

I pushed and banged on it. I couldn't open it.

I sat down in the dirt.

Think . . . My friends are upstairs, and a spaceship is coming to take them away, and I'm down here trapped in a tunnel under an insane asylum on a stupid planet because I'm so smart.

Not smart enough, not bad enough. What a dumb jerk you are, always thinking you're smarter and badder than everybody else, and when it really matters, you mess up big-time.

Stop whining. When the going gets tough, the tough get going.

If this is the tunnel to the guardhouse, I could try to escape from the guardhouse. But what could I do out there? How would I get back to help everybody?

What should I do?

Don't cry.

I did the only other thing I could think of to do. I did it to give myself courage. I took out my fiddle and started to play.

I played my half of the dueling violins from *Riverdance*.

Ten times. I didn't care who heard me, even if it was Duke or Earl or Dr. Traum. I was like a crazy person myself.

I finished, exhausted, and dropped to the dirt. Suddenly, I heard an echo far away of violin strings zinging and popping.

Only it wasn't an echo.

It was the other half of the duet.

Dad's half.

I jumped up and started playing, loud as I could, until the music bounced off the ceiling and walls and floor of the tunnel and surrounded me.

Dad appeared in the tunnel. He looked thinner and grayer than I remembered. But it was Dad—it was his smile, the way his eyes twinkled. I wrapped my arms around him. He hugged me around the shoulders.

Now I was crying. It was hard to get the words out. "I never thought you were dead."

"I'm sorry I put you through all this, Tommy." He bent over and put his forehead against mine.

"You had no choice. You did it to save us all."

"I had a choice, Tommy. I did it because I thought it was right. I'm not sure I had a right to make things even harder for you and Eddie."

"Sure you did. We're rebels, like you."

He squeezed me hard. When I looked at his face again, his eyes were wet.

I said, "You're an alien, aren't you?"

He laughed. "Whatever that means. Aliens don't think they're aliens."

"My real mom died."

"She was wonderful."

"So what are Eddie and me? Like, half-alien, half-human?"

"Something like that."

"Do we have, you know, powers?"

Dad nodded and said, solemnly, "You do."

"Like what?"

"You'll find out when it's time."

I said, "What are we going to do now?"

"Make a deal," said Dad. "They want me. They'll let you and Eddie and your friends go."

"Forget it! We're going to fight them together."

He kissed my forehead and rubbed my head with his knuckles. It felt good. "You're a fighter, Tommy, but this is not the time."

"What's going to happen?"

"They'll take me back to Homeplace. But there are people there who will help me escape and come back to you."

"And then what?"

"Keep doing what I've been doing. Organizing humans to save their planets. Fight global warming, fight starvation, disease, war. I've been waiting for you and Eddie to join me and start a revolution of kids saving the Earths."

"Eddie started already. Tech Off! Day."

"I know about that. Tell him how proud I am."

"Can't you tell him?"

"Someday I will," Dad said, smiling. "Count on it."

"Couldn't the alien scientists just fix things?"

"Maybe. But we would have to convince them that people on Earth would really change their ways and not destroy themselves and the universe along with them."

I said, "How could we do that?"

"By starting the process on the Earths." He hugged me again. "We'd better get going. You need to get back to Eddie's house. Grandpa's there."

"Am I going to see you again?"

"You'd better believe it. Now go." He pushed me toward the ladder. Together we opened the trapdoor and went upstairs.

I watched Dad walk out the front door of the asylum. Then I dug out the TPT SafecrackerPlus again. I felt sad but strong. I knew what I had to do.

SIXTY-ONE

Just before the sky went dark and a terrible roaring filled the asylum, Britzky saw a small pale face through the bars of the cell window. A kid his age, but ghostly. He couldn't tell if it was a girl or a boy. An alien? Britzky shivered, and then the entire building shivered. The huge noise sounded like a tornado. The face disappeared.

In the hallway, Duke grabbed Eddie. "Let's go. The station ship's here. C'mon, you guys." He signaled to Alessa and Britzky to follow him. "Hey . . . Where's the other twin?"

Instead of answering Duke, Eddie said to Todd, "Put a hat on him."

Britzky didn't even pause to think about it. He lowered his head and rammed into Duke's stomach. Duke slammed backward into the stone wall, headfirst, and slid down to the floor.

"You can start on my team!" yelled Eddie. "Let's go."

Britzky and Alessa followed him out into the hall and down the stairs. On the first floor they saw Tom opening cells and waving patients toward the front door. He ran to them. "There's a tunnel out of here, down a trapdoor in that room near the front door. Go. I'll meet you outside the fence."

"I'm staying with you," said Eddie.

"Me, too," said Britzky.

"No, go on. Get these people moving into the tunnel so we can get lost in the crowd and get out of here. It's what Dad wants."

Eddie froze. "Dad? You saw him? You talked to him?"

"Hurry!"

Britzky pulled Eddie and Alessa toward the front of the asylum. Through the glass door, they saw lights blinking in the blackness of the sky, red and white lights. A door in the sky slid open, and they looked up into the belly of a spaceship.

An open elevator came down. Merlyn was standing on the platform. When it reached the parking lot of the asylum, Dr. Traum stepped on. He was gripping the arm of a tall thin man with graying black hair.

"Dad!" yelled Eddie.

Dad turned and waved.

See you later, alligator.

Eddie lost his breath. *Did I imagine that?*

Alessa, Britzky, and Eddie joined a crowd of people, hundreds of them in gray pajamas, all screaming and waving their arms like rag dolls. Britzky thought they looked like crazy people. *They* are *crazy people,* he thought. *Or maybe that's just what the government wants us to believe.*

The three of them pushed the patients toward a door marked AUTHORIZED PERSONNEL ONLY. There was an open trapdoor in the floor. There was a metal ladder.

"I can't do that," said Alessa.

"You have to," said Britzky. He poked Eddie, who seemed numb. *Still thinking about his dad,* Britzky thought. "You pitch, I'll catch."

Britzky clambered down the ladder and held up his arms. Eddie shoved Alessa through the trapdoor. She yelled and squirmed, but Britzky caught her on the ladder and helped her to the dirt floor of the tunnel. *She isn't that heavy,* he thought.

They crouched and ran through the tunnel, surrounded by patients shoving and screaming and bouncing off the dirt walls. Some of them fell. Other patients stepped over them and on them. It was hot and hard to breathe. Clumps of dirt dropped from the ceiling. Alessa stumbled and Eddie staggered like a zombie, but Britzky held on to them both and pushed them along. He felt strong and proud, taking care of his friends.

The tunnel ended at another ladder. Patients were piled up at the bottom of the ladder. Britzky shoved them aside and boosted Eddie up the ladder, then Alessa. Eddie pulled while Britzky pushed from below.

They came up outside the chainlink fence. The patients here were milling around, unsure of where to go. A guard was backing away from the crowd of gray pajamas, yelling into a hand-held radio.

Britzky looked up in time to see the tall thin man waving down at them as the elevator rose into the spaceship. Dr. Traum and Merlyn were smiling. The elevator disappeared through the opening. A door slid shut.

There was a deafening noise as the spaceship began to move. There was a crash, a cracking, and then an avalanche of stones as the ship bumped into one of the towers and knocked it over.

"Look out!" yelled Alessa.

A white van was speeding toward them.

There was no place to run. The chainlink fence was opening, and guards swarmed out to herd the patients back into the building.

Suddenly, a honking horn cut through the noise. A black Cadillac roared out of the asylum parking lot.

Patients and guards scattered as the black Cadillac cut in front of the white van and came to a screeching stop next to them. Britzky saw that same small pale face peeking over the steering wheel.

Tom stuck his head out the window. "Get in!"

He opened the back door, and they piled in.

SIXTY-TWO

RONNIE felt big and powerful, as if he were the car. *Harmless little mouse. You think so?*

He could just see over the steering wheel, and his toes could barely touch the brake and the accelerator. Good thing it was one of the new automatic-transmission cars, where you didn't need to shift gears.

The four kids were hugging and hollering in the back seat.

"Uh-oh," said Tom. "The white van."

It was coming right at them.

Ronnie wrenched the wheel. The van and the Cadillac scraped as they passed. *I've got to go faster.* But when he pushed down on the accelerator with his toe, his head slipped below the level of the steering wheel and he couldn't see out the windshield. He hated to ask for help, but . . .

"Eddie, do the pedals."

Eddie somersaulted onto the front seat and then crawled down under the steering wheel, his left hand on the brake pedal, his right hand on the gas. "Got 'em."

"Hit the gas!"

The car shot ahead, and the three kids in the rear fell back screaming.

But the white van grew larger in the rearview mirror.

"It's gaining on us," said Britzky.

"More gas!" shouted Ronnie.

"The pedal's all the way down," said Eddie, his voice muffled.

They were on a highway. In the distance, Ronnie could see the skyscrapers of the city on the other side of a river. "Where are we?"

Alessa found a map in a door pocket. "Somewhere in New Jersey, but this map's no good. It's from 1957."

"Duh," said Tom. "This *is* 1957."

"Don't talk to her like that," said Britzky.

"It's okay," said Alessa. "It's Tom. He can't help it."

"And I'm right," said Tom.

Up ahead, there were construction signs. The highway narrowed to one lane. Right in front of them, a cement truck rumbled along. Behind them, the white van filled the rearview mirror.

"More gas!" yelled Ronnie. "I've got to pass this truck before the lane ends."

"Pedal's on the floor," said Eddie.

Tom said, "Pull up behind the truck."

"I'll get stuck there," said Ronnie.

"Just do it!"

"The van's right on our tail," said Britzky. "The driver's pointing at us."

"That's Earl," said Tom. "He's out for payback. It's clouding his mind."

"How do you know?" said Alessa.

"I know," said Tom.

The van tapped their rear bumper. Earl was waving at them to pull over.

Yeah, right, thought Ronnie.

Earl bumped them harder. Ronnie struggled to hold on to the steering wheel.

Tom said, "Okay, Ronnie, just as soon as it's one lane, make a hard left straight into the construction barrier."

"You sure?" said Alessa.

"It's got to be a complete surprise," said Tom. "Wait until the van gets ready to hit us again."

Ronnie cackled. "I saw this in a movie."

"I got it from a video game," said Tom. "Get up,

Eddie, and hold on to something. Everybody hold on. Now!"

The van roared up behind them. Ronnie wrenched the wheel left. Eddie uncurled himself from the floor just as the Cadillac's grille smashed into the orange and white wooden construction fence. The fence split apart.

"Look out!" yelled Britzky as the Cadillac headed off the road into a construction shed.

Ronnie slid down to hit the brake. Eddie grabbed the steering wheel and wrenched the Cadillac back onto the single lane, in front of the cement truck.

Behind them, the white van hit the cement truck and spun out of control. It skidded over the guardrail and tumbled down a hill. They heard a crash.

"Keep going!" yelled Tom.

"We should stop and help," said Eddie.

"Are you nuts?"

"Pull him out before it blows up!" said Eddie.

"Hit the gas!" yelled Tom. "Let's get out of here."

There was an explosion — fire and smoke.

"This is wrong," said Eddie.

"He's an alien," said Britzky. "He'll survive."

Ronnie pulled himself up and kneeled on the driver's seat. "Somebody take the pedals."

Britzky climbed over the seat and went down under the wheel, one hand on each pedal.

In the rearview mirror, Ronnie watched Eddie flop over into the back and curl into a ball against one of the doors. He looked terrible, eyes red, mouth open. Ronnie felt bad for him. Sometimes Eddie was just too good for his own good.

SIXTY-THREE

Maybe we killed him.

He was going to kill us.

"Are you guys sending messages to each other?" said Alessa. She was squeezed between us. "I can feel air-waves."

"Twin talk," I said. "Eddie feels bad about waxing Earl."

"Forget it," said Britzky from under the steering wheel. "We probably need to drive a stake through his heart."

"That's for a vampire," said Alessa.

I leaned back. I couldn't believe we hadn't been pulled over by the police. *Speeding, crashing through a construction site, a twelve-year-old driver who can't reach the pedals. Don't they have cops in 1957?*

"I know how to get home from here," said Eddie. "I

watched Grandpa. We went to football games in Union County."

"We went to concerts," I said.

"Different grandpas?" asked Alessa.

"Different planets," I said.

Eddie was staring out the window.

"You're thinking about Dad, aren't you?" I said.

"If you guys want to talk privately, that's okay," said Alessa.

We both said "Thanks" at the same time. She smiled. She's really not that fat.

I saw him for one second, Tommy. I imagined he said, "See you later, alligator."

He probably did. If we can talk in our heads, so can he.

You think so?

Sure, Eddie. We played a violin duet, and he didn't even have a violin.

Did you get to talk to him?

He said to tell you how proud he was about Tech Off! Day.

He knew?

He said he'd been waiting for us to join him to fight global warming and starvation and war. He talked about a revolution of kids saving the planets.

I must have been talking out loud because Alessa said, "I could get behind that," and from under the wheel Britzky said, "Sign me up."

"Me, too," said Ronnie. "What's going to happen to your dad?"

"He said that they'll take him to their planet. But that he'll escape and come back here."

"He can do that," said Alessa. "He's a monitor, right?"

Eddie said, "He quit."

"Do you guys have special powers?" asked Britzky.

"He said we'll find out when it's time," I said.

Eddie leaned back and closed his eyes. "You really think we'll ever see him again?"

"Bet on it, bro," I said, trying to sound more confident than I felt.

Eddie was crying. Alessa put an arm around him, and then she started crying. I let the tears go, too.

SIXTY-FOUR

NEARMONT, N.J.
1957

NEARMONT in 1957 looked both the same and different to Alessa. There were fewer houses and more farms. Downtown was pretty much the same, although there was a miniature golf course where the IGA would be, and the Verizon store was a crafts shop. There were fields where the high school and the nursing home would eventually go.

"Take a left here," said Eddie. "Second driveway."

When Ronnie turned into the driveway, a dog came racing out.

"Buddy!" screamed Eddie, jumping out of the car.

The dog leaped into Eddie's arms. They rolled around on the lawn, kissing each other.

"Eeeeuw," said Alessa.

"That dog tried to bite me," said Tom.

"I wonder why," said Alessa.

Ronnie climbed out of the car and ran to Eddie and Buddy, who stopped licking Eddie's face long enough to give Ronnie a lick.

"What's going on?" said Britzky, climbing up from under the steering wheel. He was red and sweaty.

"You were terrific, Todd," said Alessa.

"Well, um, just doing my job." He looked happy. "What happens now?"

An old guy came out of the house. Tom and Eddie ran to him. Ronnie, too.

"Must be Grandpa," said Alessa.

"Whose?" said Britzky.

"Both of them, if they're twins," said Alessa. She smiled at Britzky's scrunched face. "I don't get it a hundred percent, either."

Grandpa came over to shake their hands. "You kids did great."

"We're the seventh grade version of the Justice League of America," said Britzky. He grinned when Alessa punched his arm.

"After my time," said Grandpa. He looked at his wristwatch. "Say your goodbyes. I've got to get you back home."

"Group hug," said Alessa. She was crying again.

Eddie and Tom put their foreheads together. Ronnie and Britzky shook hands. Britzky said, "You should be a Nascar driver, dude."

"If you do my pedals, Big Daddy."

Alessa felt sad as Grandpa herded them all back into the car. They were quiet on the drive to the field where the nursing home would someday stand. Tom, Alessa, and Britzky stood near a tree while Grandpa adjusted the dials of a small black box.

"It's not over," he said. "We'll all meet again."

He pressed a button.

SIXTY-FIVE

THE team cheered when the old football coach showed up at practice. No one had liked Dr. Traum. One of the linemen said, "He was like a creepy alien from outer space."

Everybody laughed except Eddie.

The old school psychologist came back, too. He sent for Eddie. "These unexplained absences," he said. "Anything wrong?"

Eddie wanted to ask the guy about *his* unexplained absences. How had Dr. Traum managed to take over? Some kind of alien mind control? But he just shook his head, which was a mistake. The headache came back. "I'm fine."

"Glad to hear that, Eddie. The team needs you."

Eddie stayed busy, with the team and being boy

leader of the school drive to collect canned goods for starving children. Another girl took over Merlyn's job as girl leader. Merlyn didn't come back to school.

The last few days sometimes seemed like a fantasy story. Had they really happened? *It could have been a dream from getting my bell rung,* Eddie thought. Sometimes he wondered if he wanted it to be a dream. He hated the thought of Dad being a prisoner on another planet. He felt guilty about killing Earl, even though he was an evil guy.

But if it *was* a dream, he would never see Tom and Dad again.

And if it was a dream, what was Dr. Traum's black Cadillac doing in the garage? Grandpa kept the garage door locked, and he even painted over the little windows on the overhead sliding door so no one could see the car. Someday, Grandpa said, the car would come in handy, but until then it had to be a secret.

Eddie stopped thinking it had all been a dream when two FBI agents showed up at school to ask him how he knew about *Sputnik*. Was he getting messages from the Russians? It took him a few minutes to figure out it must have been a Tom thing. Eddie wanted to say, *That wasn't me—it was my brother from another planet.* But he figured you don't crack wise to G-men. After a while, the school psychologist and the football coach convinced the agents that it must have been something the weird Dr. Traum had cooked up.

Ronnie was nervous. "Do you think we'll ever see Tom and your dad again?"

"Better believe it. Why are you so jumpy?"

Ronnie looked around to be sure no one could hear. "I keep seeing Earl's face through windows, even at school. Like he's a ghost haunting me for killing him."

When Eddie told Grandpa about that, Grandpa invited Ronnie to live with them. Eddie was surprised when Ronnie hemmed and hawed. He wasn't sure about moving in. Eddie wondered if the little guy wanted to be free, but it turned out he wanted his privacy. When Grandpa said he could sleep in the finished basement and use the bathroom and shower down there, Ronnie looked very happy.

"Remember," said Grandpa. "There's no such thing as ghosts. Earl's not dead. The monitors sent him to watch us. They think we'll try to rescue John."

"We will," said Eddie and Ronnie together.

Grandpa smiled. "You bet your life."

SIXTY-SIX

I WAS Mr. Tech Off! It felt bogus to be famous for something that Eddie had done. Everybody thought it was such a great idea. Mrs. Rupp called it a "teachable moment," which meant that she talked about it until it was boring. And then we didn't talk about it anymore.

But the more I thought about it, the more I liked the idea. Dad had liked it. It was part of the revolution he talked about. My job was to carry on what Eddie started, and both of us had to carry on what Dad started. And to think about what else we could do to save the planets, to be real rebels.

I tried to talk to Dad the way I talked to Eddie, but I never tuned in his voice. Maybe Homeplace was too far away. Maybe the other aliens had blocked transmission. Sometimes when I played my half of the *Riverdance* duet, I thought I heard his half. But that could be imagination.

Alessa, Britzky, and I talked all the time about what had happened. That never got boring. Britzky kept reminding us that Dr. Traum had called us the seventh grade version of the Justice League of America. Dr. Traum had been sarcastic, Alessa said, but Britzky loved the idea. He even laughed when I said he could be the superhero Bratman.

"Lessi can be Wonder Woman, and you and Eddie can take turns being Superman."

"What about Ronnie?" said Alessa.

"Robin," said Britzky.

"Who's that?" asked Alessa.

"Batman used to have a sidekick, a kid named Robin."

"What happened to him?" asked Alessa.

"Child labor laws," I said.

Mom and the Lump never asked about the time I was gone. I think they know more than they let on, but I don't want to talk about any of it with them. I know Mom would have liked to hear about Dad, but I was still angry at her for not telling me about my birth mom. Alessa says I've got to just get over it. I guess I will.

The Lump was almost back to being his usual jerk self. Almost. Sometimes I caught him looking at me with a little smile on his ugly face. Britzky thought that if the Lump really did work for the government, he was part of the alien program. I'll keep an eye on him. I still have his private number but I haven't hacked into it yet. Meanwhile, we have that truce he wanted.

Grandpa was back in the nursing home, playing senile. When I tried to ask him why, since the monitors must know he's faking, he pretended he didn't understand. I figure he knows what he's doing.

SIXTY-SEVEN

How you hangin', Tomski?

Okay. I think about Dad all the time.

At least you got to be with him. That was the ginchiest.

Do you have to talk like that?

Like what?

Skip it. Are you still seeing Earl?

Every few days. I'm glad he's not dead, but it gives me and Ronnie the willies.

They must be worried we'll try to rescue Dad.

That's what Grandpa says.

We have to figure a way to get to Homeplace.

There must be a tech thing you can figure out.

Gotta be. The Bratman wants to try. Alessa, too.

Ronnie's on deck. But how would we do it?

Have you talked to Grandpa about it?

He says to cool my jets. We'll know when the time comes.

Is Merlyn back in your school?

No. Yours?

No.

I'd better go. Grandpa thinks they're still monitoring us.

See you later, alligator.

After a while, crocodile. Wish I'd said that to Dad.

The stars blinked off.

SIXTY-EIGHT

ALESSA, Britzky, and I sometimes talk about how boring Nearmont and school seem now. We're working on the election campaign that Alessa started with Eddie, but that's not enough to float my boat. Not after what we've been through.

I'm having an easier time than I ever thought I would talking to kids, mostly about technology and global warming and how there are hungry people, even in America. It feels like we're starting the revolution. Dad's revolution.

Britzky says I'm different now, friendlier, more like Eddie. I don't feel different. The old orchestra teacher came back, and after he gave Alessa a hard time about her weak technique—pushing the bow with her forearm—I mime-walked behind him in the auditorium during an assembly. Crowd went wild. He turned and saw it and busted me into the second violin section. *Big whoop.*

Sometimes we wonder if there's anybody we should tell our story to, like Homeland Security or the FBI, so they could go after the aliens. But Alessa thinks they wouldn't believe us and would lock us up. Britzky thinks they *would* believe us, because they already know, and would lock us up.

As time goes on, we need to keep reminding each other that it all happened. We have little reminders. I got Britzky and Alessa reading Mark Twain books. It's spooky how you can find connections in *The Prince and the Pauper* and *A Connecticut Yankee in King Arthur's Court* with things that happened on the twin Earths. Alessa thinks Mark Twain had a great imagination. Britzky thinks Mark Twain might have been a monitor.

Britzky and I started playing Chinese handball at lunch against a wall of the school. Other kids got into it. Some are pretty good. Some of the Asian kids didn't like the name, so we changed it to Ace-King-Queen, Duke's name for the game. Even girls play.

The basketball coach begs me to come out for the team. I want to tell him, *You don't want me, you want my brother from another planet.* But I just lie and say that I'm preparing for a big violin competition and don't have time. Actually, I don't have a lot of free time. I'm working on the CloakIII and a more powerful version of the pepper spray bomb that blew up in Earl's face in the park. I just got the new TPT GreaseShot V. It has *three* settings.

I think about Dad all the time. I believe what Grandpa on EarthTwo said: "It's not over. We'll all meet again."

While we're waiting, there's plenty to do right here on Earth. Both of them.

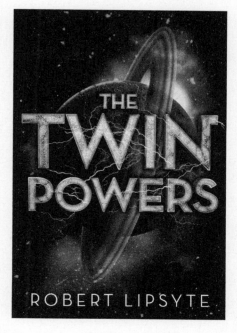

ONE

THE aliens came back in the spring, just when I was beginning to think I'd never see Dad or my identical twin brother, Eddie, again. For years I had thought Eddie was imaginary, a voice in my head. When he came to Earth, a real live brother, it was one of the best days of my life. I thought we'd find Dad together and crack the mystery of just who we were.

It had been six months since we'd watched Dad disappear into the belly of the aliens' spaceship. I hadn't talked to Eddie in weeks. What was there to talk about? We were stuck on different planets—him on EarthTwo in 1958 and me on EarthOne in 2012—and nothing much had been happening on either one.

The day it all started again, I was ghosting through my morning classes, feeling down. Even Mrs. Rupp, the dumb history teacher with her boring timeline, couldn't get my juices going. She was on a topic that should have been interesting—nuclear energy—but Mrs. Rupp made us waste our time memorizing dates instead of learning stories that could explain why things happened. Usually I interrupt her because I'm bad, a troublemaker who likes to shake things up. I can't stand bullies or know-it-alls, even if they're teachers. But that day I kept my mouth shut. That's how down I felt. My best friends, Alessa and Britzky, thought I was sick.

At lunch, I hesitated before sitting at our regular table in the far corner of the cafeteria by the garbage cans, what I called the rebel table because we dared to be different. I didn't want to be around Alessa and Britzky. They reminded me of everything I had hoped would happen but hadn't yet—the three of us, plus Eddie and his sidekick, Ronnie, plus Dad and Grandpa together again on our mission to save the Earths from destruction. If the Earths didn't destroy themselves first by nuclear explosions or extreme weather, then the aliens would wipe us out. They were sure that the Earths would destabilize the entire universe—including them!

What made it even more complicated was that Dad and Grandpa were aliens and Eddie and I were half alien. Maybe the world's only halfies.

Maybe it was time to get thrown out of school again, I thought. I could start my fourth middle school! I wondered if that would be a Guinness World Record.

When I did sit down, Britzky poked me. I poked him back without looking at him until he said, "Check out this dude."

The chatter and clatter of the cafeteria had faded away. Teachers had stopped talking on their phones. The kids at the jock, fashion, drama, digital, social, thug, and toasted tables were silent.

The only sound was the clop of boots as a short, pale kid in a long black raincoat that flapped against his black jeans marched slowly toward us.

There was no expression on his face. He reminded me of someone. *Who?* I thought he was looking directly at me but I couldn't be sure because of the old-fashioned aviator shades he was wearing.

I whispered to Alessa and Britzky, "I thought you're not allowed to wear dark glasses in school."

"He's new," said Alessa, who worked in the school secretary's office. "His records are sealed."

"That means he just got out of juvie," said Britzky, his usually loud voice soft. "Or he's a government informer."

I thought of a third possibility. I wondered if they were thinking it, too.

Alessa said, "His name is Hercules."

"What kind of name is that?" I said.

Britzky whispered, "That could mean something. In the book *A Connecticut Yankee in King Arthur's Court,* the guy who hits the hero over the head is nicknamed Hercules. And you know how the aliens love books by Mark Twain."

So Britzky *was* thinking about what I was thinking about. *Aliens!*

Hercules kept coming toward us. I wondered what he was covering up under his raincoat. Seventh-graders didn't carry automatic weapons into school. Not yet, anyway.

As usual, I was ready to rumble. That's the way I am. I felt for my Extreme-Temperature Narrow-Beam Climate Simulators. I had never used them in combat. They were two Sharpie-size nano composite rods. Scientists had invented them as part of the battle against global warming, but the Army was interested in using them as weapons. So was I. I'd hacked the data and built them myself. They were my new favorite personal weapons. The data claimed either rod could stop a water buffalo. Together they could stop a herd. This might be a chance to see what the rods could do.

Hercules halted a few feet from the table. His voice was familiar. "Which one of you freaks is Tom Canty?"

Britzky jumped up and got between us. "What do you want with Tom?" He was in his old bodyguard mode. "You'll have to deal with me first."

"Ah, the paranoid loudmouth Britzky," said Hercules.

How did he know about Britzky? "As Mark Twain said, 'It's better to keep your mouth shut and be thought a fool than to open it and remove all doubt.'"

The pimples on Britzky's forehead went neon, the way they always do when he's mad. He lowered his head but kept his eyes on Hercules and charged.

Hercules lifted his shades and stared at him with bright green eyes. We had seen such eyes before. They were alien eyes. Britzky froze, then turned around and walked back to his seat.

Hercules lowered his shades and turned to me. "So you must be the famous Tom Canty."

I stood up. "I'm Tom Canty."

Hercules smiled. "The YouTube star himself?"

The YouTube clip had gotten me kicked out of my second middle school. I had put a bully on his butt in the cafeteria with a blast from my TPT GreaseShot, my favorite weapon the year before. Someone had recorded the action with an iPhone and it was all over the Internet in seconds.

"Are you the Tom Canty who people mistakenly think founded Tech Off! Day?"

Mistakenly? How could he know that? It was my twin, Eddie, who'd come up with Tech Off! Day, in which everybody was supposed to switch off all electronic devices for one day and get to know other people face-to-face. This had been last fall, when Eddie was on my planet pretending to be me and I was on his planet pretending to be him. Being Eddie wasn't easy for me. He's a nice guy.

But only the seven of us—me, Eddie, Alessa, Britzky, Ronnie, Grandpa, and Dad—plus the aliens—knew about the switch. Why had the aliens sent down this creepy guy? His green eyes meant he was an alien, too.

"What do you want, Hercules?" I showed him some attitude. All around the cafeteria, kids were pointing their phones and tablets at us.

"I hear you think you're bad," said Hercules. "I've come to find out how bad."

ROBERT LIPSYTE was an award-winning sports-writer for the *New York Times* and the Emmy-winning host of the nightly public affairs show *The Eleventh Hour*. He is the author of more than a dozen acclaimed novels for young adults and is the recipient of the Margaret A. Edwards Award honoring his lifetime contribution in that genre. He has also written numerous works of fiction and nonfiction for adults. He lives in Manhattan and on Shelter Island, New York, with his wife, Lois Morris, and his dog, Milo. Visit his website at **www.robertlipsyte.com**.